Kazu

Daniel Buckman served as a paratrooper with the U.S. Army's 82nd Airborne Division. *Because the Rain* is his fourth novel.

DANIEL BUCKMAN

BECAUSE
the RAIN

PICADOR

ST. MARTIN'S PRESS

NEW YORK

BECAUSE THE RAIN. Copyright © 2007 by Daniel Buckman. All rights reserved. Printed in the United States of America. No part of this book may be used or reproduced in any manner whatsoever without written permission except in the case of brief quotations embodied in critical articles or reviews. For information, address Picador, 175 Fifth Avenue, New York, N.Y. 10010.

www.picadorusa.com

Picador® is a U.S. registered trademark and is used by St. Martin's Press under license from Pan Books Limited.

For information on Picador Reading Group Guides, please contact Picador.
E-mail: readinggroupguides@picadorusa.com

The first chapter of this novel previously.appeared in different form in *Chicago Noir,* edited by Neal Pollack and published by Akashic Books in 2005.

Library of Congress Cataloging-in-Publication Data

Buckman, Daniel, 1967–
     Because the rain / Daniel Buckman.
          p. cm.
     ISBN-13: 978-0-312-42763-4
     ISBN-10: 0-312-42763-8
     1. Chicago (Ill.)—Fiction. 2. Vietnam War, 1961–1975—Veterans—Fiction.
3. Vietnamese—Illinois—Chicago—Fiction. 4. Prostitutes—Fiction. I. Title.

PS3602.U27B43 2007
813'.6—dc22

2006051180

First published in the United States by St. Martin's Press

First Picador Edition: February 2008

10 9 8 7 6 5 4 3 2 1

In memory of Jack Daniel Pomon
1980–2003

The pure products of America go crazy.
—*William Carlos Williams*

BECAUSE
the RAIN

1

The rain streamed off the porch roof and the black sheets dissolved Chicago and they thought themselves behind a waterfall. Mike put his hand on Susan's cheek, her hair windblown against his knuckles. She held her breath and they bit each other's lips. After twelve years, it was what they did to make things feel new. But the rain kept coming, beating the leaves from the maples and the elms, turning the gutters into rivulets floating Starbucks pastry bags.

They went upstairs to lie down and the rain fell harder with the late darkness. He held his wife against him, her back warm and damp. She felt the rain through the screen, more than he did, and pushed into his chest until he moved. There had been long days of rain and they never knew the rain from the sky. If the sunlight came, it showed hard before the dusk, and made the streets steam. But there were two weeks before they would talk about the wet summer, a month before the rains ruined July with low, gray skies.

Mike Spence had told Susan he was going to be a cop over delivered Thai food. His academy class was starting in three months down on Monroe by Rico's, where they once drank vodka martinis, singing Dean Martin songs with a bartender friendly over past tips and watching the fall outs from the police trainee runs spit and hold their sides. Who the hell could they chase, he'd laughed. No soldier would lower himself to be a cop. Now, he was thirty-five, a paratrooper discharged fourteen years ago, and he hadn't won a thing.

I wrote a book about me, he thought. Winners and losers. That was the risk.

"You'll stay a year," his wife said.

"I start in ninety days."

"I don't think it's what you want."

She sat up and drew the bedsheet around her breasts and pointed in his face. He looked out the window. A writer, he was thinking. Just because that idea moved him didn't mean it was moving. He felt crazy sometimes, even undone, like he'd been climbing hard but the ladder was up against the wrong wall. In the early darkness, her eyes searched his face.

"Why do you still get this way," she said.

"I'm no one way anymore," he said.

"You get these ideas," she said, "but life isn't a story. You were just talking about going to Iraq with Quakers. Last year, you were going to backpack through Cambodia. You always attach yourself to something that is not your own."

He looked at her and then at themselves in the wall mirror. Her biceps were bruised from wrestling with autistic boys from her special education class. In grocery stores, people eyed her arms and stared at him while she scanned cat food and mangoes through the self-checkout. A dyke is going to hit you someday, she'd laugh. Just leave you for dead.

"You're not a character," she said.

"You don't know?" he said.

"I know you're not a character."

Mike Spence listened to the rain. He knew his wife saw a bloated cop parked in the wagon outside a 7-Eleven while his partner got a coffee and eyed the Indian girl's breasts. Pooja, she'd be thinking. My husband's partner will be eyeing Pooja.

Later, in his shaded room, Mike read his work when Susan was quiet outside the door, listening. There were noises she made, noises she thought he didn't hear, the way she coughed from breathing slowly through her nose, the floor creak from her shifting weight. As a kind of game, he made his voice like slick rocks, doing Barry White, Al Green, Isaac Hayes. He tried making her laugh, breaking her cover, but she was silent. The abortion had been the price to keep his life, not hers. It was making her eyes hard. A cop, she'd said. After we did it for you to write. He forgot her coughing between the fan creaks and read in the bulb light.

I saw these guys who looked like Todds in the Loop after rush hour. I gave them last names.

Todd Miller. Todd Turner. Todd Stevens.

They were always squinting from the white heat still glinting off bus windows. Six thirty was the earliest I ever watched them leave the First National Building, humping the sidewalk in the white heat of summer, swinging a briefcase up Dearborn Street, then long-stepping among the women with popcorn in the Picasso's shadow. Todd's father taught him how to stay low and know how much things cost. He kept a fraction in his head and headed to the El after ten hours at Sidley and Austin, jamming down the subway stairs slick from spilled popcorn. He moved like a golden retriever and loosened his tie. Humiliation for Todd was going from wild-caught sockeye salmon at Whole Foods to the flash-frozen farm-raised fish Costco lets you buy if you pay the fifty dollars a year. He had to ask Jennifer to eat that, look her in those swim-team blue eyes and say things were weird at work.

I wrote a book about my having been a soldier for Todd. He needed to see drunken barracks fights on the weekends, know what he missed when Jacky Bozak and Ernie Chopper threw hands, strung out on crank and Michelob, and my best friend Edward Dilger had Charge of Quarters after the top sergeants went home to duplexes and house trailers. I didn't hold back for Todd. He read how Dilger beat his knuckles bloody on Bozak's plate face, himself a new corporal and six months to discharge, but couldn't make the wired Pollack stop choking the hillbilly. Todd couldn't leave this earth, suddenly and beautifully with Jennifer in the collapse of a Whole Foods parking lot, and not experience Bozak's frozen skull take Dilger's punches. It was like watching a sledge head begin breaking up concrete. Chopper strained to keep his eyes open while his lips went dark.

I waited at Whole Foods meat counters after the novel came out and bought chicken while Todd picked free-range T-bones, his hand cart heavy from organic artichoke hearts in cans. He wore fleeces and suede slipper walking shoes and I knew he'd mess himself if Dilger even aimed his eyes at him and got cold. Edward Dilger taught himself to have still eyeballs by shooting coyotes with a .223 Ruger for the twenty-dollar bounty in Tom Hall County, Texas. Todd never watched a guy like Dilger get dragged off by two MPs for having punched Bozak too long, until his eye hung sideways, and he collapsed against Chopper's back and dripped blood on his shaved head.

Todd never paid twenty-two dollars to know about guys like my buddy. He did pay dearly for chicken breasts already rubbed with herbs. The army paid Dilger and Sidley paid Todd. The guy couldn't see the problem.

I'd written about how Dilger was a good soldier but when the MP sticked him by the stairs, four of his teeth bounced off the cinder-block walls like pellets. The CO took his stripes three days later for not calling the MPs first thing. Todd couldn't be human unless he saw Dilger in Key West two years after the army, Dilger making manhattans at Sloppy Joes, and knew that he'd started shooting speed under his tongue. But Todd probably had some college friend whose parent committed suicide junior year, just after a year in England, and finding Dilger dead in his apartment bathroom didn't shock him. He loaned heavy for Northwestern Law School and didn't spare cash for other people's pain. If he died tomorrow in the collapse of the Whole Foods parking lot, he'd sleep forever in his Range Rover like the pharaohs in mountain tombs.

In May, after the abortion, Mike and Susan drove Interstate 80 from Chicago to the Rocky Mountains. They rented an old timbered cabin in the pines at the bottom of Estes Canyon. There was good shade from the trees and there was a fast stream coming down from the mountains and a narrow gravel road that dropped steeply from the highway and stopped in the jagged black stumps at the bank below the cabin. There were cottages up the highway, circled by birches, and if there were people, they did not see them. It was early in the season and very cold and rainy at night.

The stream came straight from the Continental Divide, where water became other water, all powerful and cold, but the trout were gone from the shallows and they could not drink the water any more than they could from the Chicago River. If they'd not sent the deposit, he would have left over it. An alpine stream, the Internet ad read, cold, clear snow runoff. He assumed he could dip his cupped hand and drink sloppily, letting the water numb his mouth, but the rental manager dropped off two cases of Evian for the week. Screw this place, Mike said. But Susan calmed him, the way she did after the happiness about his first novel faded like a new car smell. She made him look north where the woods and the canyon walls were all one thing, like a great idea, strangely jagged and soft, but always the same. They were here to let go. They were here to wash it all away and see if they could feel clean again. Relax, she told him. She lowered her voice to say it.

At night, they wrapped themselves in one blanket and sat watching the clouds blow down from the high range. The sky turned green and the lightning splayed like fingers. They tried to make love and it went badly so they held hands and talked about getting new cats and perhaps their own house in the cornfields south of Chicago. They talked like they believed the abortion was not the sad and humiliating thing it truly was. They were cautious with each other. They never talked about the bad dreams or the weak feeling that went to their knees. Sitting still under the blanket, they would make themselves laugh by naming the new cats after cartoon characters or friends they'd had. When the jokes went, they listened to the slackening rain, holding each other, both seeing him in the waiting room with *People* magazine while she lay dilated before the doctor. Then later, when the clouds blew through the canyon, they would decide the farmhouse they wanted must have white clapboards and a long front porch and stained glass in the eastern windows to color the sunrise. I'll build a fireplace from river rocks, he said. I'll cut the wood, good hackberry. She lay her head against his shoulder, her hair wet from the leaky awning. I'll sweep the porch and try not to wake the sleeping cats, she said.

All week they held hands and hiked trails of slate rock slick from the wet spring. They came upon elk herds sleeping in scrub meadows, ground squirrels running between holes like vaudeville comics, and one night watched a coyote nosing by the car. They stopped and studied waterfalls, shooting rapids, boulders dropped among birch trees like monoliths. She took pictures, holding the camera up and down to get in his height. We pick up from here, she said. One day after the next, he thought. Like walking.

They took Interstate 80 home through the stout hills of Nebraska where cattle herds balded pastures and fat kids with sunburned legs waved from overpasses. The sunlight was low and even and white. Susan found new stations when the distance beat the signal. Outside Cheyenne, they heard Joy Division's "Love Will Tear Us Apart" on college radio, and listened through the static. He wished they could sing it together, let go the way dogs howl.

"I can't believe they're playing this song," she said.

"Go with it," he said.

"I didn't like it then."

She turned down the volume and he heard the wind over the sad, growly singer. Ian Curtis was a put-on, she said. She'd talked about dancing in the aisles at Talking Heads's concerts back in college, really throwing her arms above her head, and for twelve years he tried imagining it.

Mike first saw people scrubbing their windshields with green pads at a truck stop near Kimball. The insect guts darkened the glass like window tint, but his remained clean enough to see Susan's reflection without spots shadowed on her face. They must have hit an odd stretch of air, he thought. Smiling guys with RVs stood upon stepladders and worked their elbows, watching Susan walk for the restroom, her hand squeezing her purse strap. Look at the ass on her, their faces said.

"You can't get the bugs all the way off with a squeegee," a man in a cowboy hat told him. "Not out here. Go get you some green pads at the Wal-Mart in Brownson."

Mike nodded that he'd make do and the man shrugged his shoulders. He went looking for Susan because that morning she'd cried on a Texaco toilet seat outside Cheyenne, sobbing so hard her eyes were still swollen at noon. He'd stood outside the door, his shadow broken on a propane tank, asking her what she wanted from him. My eyes are all puffy, she'd said.

"Remember," the man called out, "it's the bugs' world in Nebraska and we just live in it."

Mike drove off and set the cruise at eighty-five and read the mileage sign for North Platte, Kearny, Omaha. Sure, Tex, he thought of the man. It's probably just like you say.

Ogallala was a hundred miles away when the bugs came out of the white sky like spilled coffee. They stitched the windshield. He looked hard through the smears and heard them hitting while Susan searched the radio for a stronger station. He couldn't see and the bug shadows spotted her cheeks. She scanned and listened for a half second, caring more about a clear signal than the music.

In Chicago, they went on dates again. Just the two of them. They were making steps, like they talked about in the mountains, and meeting at restaurant bars, the same places from ten years ago, an Italian place on Racine, or a Lebanese bistro far north on Clark. Then, they'd drunk martinis because people were doing it again, he Stoli, she Absolut, and laughed about inside jokes with friends they last knew had moved to Seattle. Lance was Heineken, then Bombay and tonic when he bloated. Elizabeth liked Cosmopolitans. It was the pretty glass, the faded red vodka. In those days, they were all just off work, the Loop or the near North Side, where women swung Coach bags and pigeon feathers fell in the puddles. They sang Nat King Cole songs with the jukebox and thought things were one big wave.

Tonight, Mike and Susan ordered their martinis and sat alone at Rico's. The bar was clean, but scratched. She played with her olive stick. Mike wanted to tell her there wasn't enough air in their apartment for two, and it was good they left the place to fill back up. Open windows, a hard wind, the curtains pushed to the ceiling. But she would only look at him, her eyes becoming wet. We were just in Colorado for two weeks, she'd say. Air isn't the problem. Now, they sat where they once drank grappa like they knew something special, and said nothing about him becoming a cop. She was sure he'd pull the plug, that it was already an old idea he had of himself. You wait, he thought. I can't lose in that world.

Mike watched the waiters watch the six o'clock news. There was a fire west on Harrison, around Cicero, an eight-flat lit up like a wedding party. Kids aped for the news camera.

"You think Lance and Elizabeth ever married?" he said.

"No. She left him for a doctor."

"How do you know?"

She pointed to the restroom through a doorway, by a pay phone. Two busboys looked at her where they folded silverware into cloth napkins.

"We used to talk in there. She was scared Lance's dreams were too tied up with him going out."

"He wanted to design computer games."

"She said he only ever had plans on bar stools beside you."

"He knew what he wanted to do."

"I bet the doctor dumped her after she left Lance."

"Where's this coming from?"

"That girl was like a monkey with men," she said. "She always had her hand on a branch before she swung. One had to break."

"You want to get a table?"

"You really thought Elizabeth was something."

"Maybe we should finish our drinks here."

"Whatever you want to do."

"She was our friend."

"He was your friend. Women make the best of being stuck together."

Mike kept quiet and drank, letting the cold vodka numb his gums before he swallowed. He was happy Susan usually stopped herself before listing the things she endured to be his wife.

Later, he left Susan lying awake and ran the city dark with an open smile. He caught the raindrops in his mouth and sprinted between the rat-proof garbage cans while the garages dissolved from the rain. He felt good, he'd drunk light, and the shoes were taking the shock while he hit puddles behind used car lots and donut shops with chained Dumpsters. The clouds sopped up the city lights. He stretched his legs and he felt only the cold rain stinging his throat.

Back home, he stood in the bedroom doorway, sweat and rain wet. His wife lay in the TV light with the cat lying across her leg. When she'd first heard him, she started making sobbing noises, though now, she was done with that. He knew she'd tried crying, but stopped after her ducts gave no water. On their third date she'd cried as badly, telling him about her college abortion over vodka tonics and T-bones beneath the Sinatra painting at Rosebud on Taylor Street.

"Six miles in forty-one minutes tonight," he said. His running shorts were stuck to his thighs.

Susan said nothing, her eyes sad and dry. He still found them beautiful, like chocolate syrup, the way he told his buddies after their first hook-up, but now, after twelve years, her brown eyes demanded an emotional admission he was afraid to stop paying because his buddies were all gone.

"Forty-one minutes," he said again. "I'll sleep through the police academy. Remember at Rico's when we'd watch the fat trainee cops run down Racine?"

Susan was silent. Mike wanted to put his finger in her face, but he didn't. She looked at the cat while she stroked its cheekbone. He knew he couldn't touch his wife even if he put his hand on her mouth.

One day, he'd remind her they were from different towns, but the same Illinois with brown rivers and cornfields running to the sky. He needed to get that straight again, remind Susan of her limitations.

"I know Harvard accepted you senior year of high school," he'd tell her. "You wrote an essay on Freud and dreams for a contest, then presented it to the Rotary Club in a long dress. You had slides of diagrams and spoke into a microphone. The bored, gray men sat in folding chairs with their legs crossed."

Susan would shake her head. Her eyes might blear while her finger pointed at his nose.

"You have no idea," she'd tell him. "There is no way you could know a thing."

"The day the envelope came," he'd say, "you saw the rain dance on pickup hoods parked among the clapboard houses. The gutters were high with muddy water from the flooded fields. You held the letter and watched the weather coming over the interstate, the paper flecking wet, knowing your mother would worry all night about the creek rising behind the house. You cried with closed eyes, alone beneath the willow tree, happy you could blame your wet face on the rain."

"I didn't see any of it. Not the way you say."

Mike told his wife nothing. He only watched her look away and rub the cat's ear between her thumb and forefinger. He knew they liked fighting more than understanding, and because of it, they'd forced each other away. She was there for the cat, not him, and he could feel good about that if he let himself. Either way, he'd jog different alleys tomorrow night, dreaming he could run until the dawn broke over the two-flat roofs, the morning light coming fast, chalky, then the palest blue.

2

Donald Goetzler stood by the long window while the rain sliced their reflected faces in the glass. Shapeless men and women lined out the conference-room door and took paper plates when they neared the food table. It was Goetzler's retirement lunch, the regulation catered buffet on Weber Industrial Supply, the long trays brought in by Mexicans in red windbreakers with their names sewn on front. The secretaries got him a white cake from a supermarket bakery. He looked at his watch, a gold Rolex date timer, then back out the window.

Weber retired Goetzler with a phone call to set up the short meeting where he'd sign for his package: one year's salary, a two-year consulting retainer, and the right to pay for group health insurance. What's your timetable, they said. He held the phone to his ear. He pressed it close, then closer, until the voice sounded like no voice at all. A fax came in. The printer spat paper. He wished he'd been tougher.

Yesterday, when he cleaned out his cubicle, he threw away three million dollars' worth of research, two years of sixty-hour weeks, inquiries into how they might get Ford and General Motors to buy their safety equipment and lightbulbs.

Shred it, they told him. We're changing our focus.

They wanted to sell hammers and light motors to prisons, federal agencies, city water departments.

The secretaries in their floral dresses looked up from the buffet where they poured ranch dressing on carrot sticks. Ari Feldman was moving through them like a cocky house cat, his paper plate sagging from the pizza slices and the stuffed shells. He was fat, his loafer heels worn into an inside slant, his XXL oxford coming untucked from his khakis with the elastic waistband. They stared squint-eyed through their glasses, looking at Feldman and the emptied pizza boxes, while he stacked garlic bread upon two oatmeal cookies. They mouthed jerk and shook their heads. He worked in quantitative market research, and e-mailed classmates from the University of Chicago about his folk rock band, The Bagel Chips. He went back and got another paper plate because the grease was leaking and wiped his hand on a chair back. He then walked right up to Goetzler, half the pizza on his plate.

"Ed Marx got a better retirement package than you did," he said.

Goetzler looked out the window.

"He got three years full pay and a five-year consulting deal," Feldman said.

"They never call them back," Goetzler said.

"They'll call Marx. He was something around here."

Goetzler looked at the sterno heating the stuffed shells. He'd stood next to some of the men at the urinals, but the women were floral dresses to him. In the window Goetzler saw that Feldman was still talking, his face blurred by the rain.

"Ed Marx got an IT degree at night before people even had the Internet. He knows trends."

Feldman was taking pizza bites before swallowing his mouthful.

"That guy is far from done. Ed Marx will be the consultant of this industry."

"You hear anybody talk about him since he left?"

"No."

"You'll get the call one day," he said.

Ari Feldman started chewing very quickly. Goetzler could see his red wet teeth.

"You stayed in the army after Vietnam," Feldman said. "I started ten years before you. I'll be a director like Ed Marx."

Goetzler pointed to the plate of pizza.

"But your ass won't fit his seat," he said.

Feldman looked away before Goetzler turned. They both watched the rain and the wind melt their reflections in the window. Feldman was burrowing his eyes into the glass while Goetzler smiled and looked at his gold Rolex date timer. He liked the way it slid from his shirt cuff. If he looked at the watch and nothing else, he could be very happy with himself and believe he got exactly what he wanted.

One morning in late June 1967, while the Officer Candidate School platoon crossed the monkey bars outside the chow hall, Donald Goetzler fell off for the last time. His hands were too small and he never got a good enough hold around the bars for his arms to take him across. He'd hold up the line. The cadets behind him, sweaty with momentum, kneed his backside. His blisters burst like opening eyes and he went down midway across. He knelt on all fours and the men's boots kicked his head, knocking off his horn-rim glasses. He looked for them, patting the red sand, the grit impacting his bloody blisters. When the platoon filed into chow hall, Goetzler went to the aid station, where he had his palms cleaned, and two hours later stood before Major McCally with gauze on his hands.

McCally lit a cigarette and reclined in his oak swivel chair. He put his jump boots upon the desk and Goetzler saw himself reflected in the shiny leather, his hands wrapped like amputated stumps. The major held the cigarette between his fingers, his hand ready to karate chop. He was with the Twenty-fifth Division in the Pacific, and had an autographed picture of James Jones on his desk. *I knew him in Hawaii before Pearl, he'd say of Jones. I even knew the little dark-eyed queer he turned into Pruitt. But Jimmy Jones. That book shoved it up their asses and he married a looker who only jumped writers and then he makes a million. Good on him.* McCally won a battlefield commission in Korea, six years after winning the Distinguished Service Cross on Iwo Jima, but his glory road had stopped at an Officer Candidate School training command.

The major's hair was cut close, flecks of gray upon the black. He looked at Goetzler with stiff blue eyes.

"They're drafting some real no-hopers into the line divisions," he said. "An infantry officer better be part lion tamer if he wants to make his mission in Vietnam."

Goetzler looked down at the bloody gauze.

"Flat out," the major said. "Your glasses are too thick. They'd steam up bad in-country. You'd get shot in the head. I'm transferring you to the MPs."

"Yessir."

"After this war, Goetzler," the major said, "the army is going to be full of dope. I mean it. You get yourself a plainclothes assignment. You find some of that dope and put the shitbirds away. Get you a pension."

"Yessir," Goetzler said.

"Lieutenant colonel in twenty. It's possible. You know how to read, Goetzler."

The army would go crazy with dope, but the war came first, twelve months of it. Goetzler commanded an MP platoon in Saigon and patrolled in a jeep with Sergeant First Class Stanley Olszewski. The apartments over the storefronts all had long windows with broken shutters needing paint. Olszewski wore a crew cut, carried a Remington 870 loaded with double-aught buckshot. There's too many gooks too fast here for an M-16, he said. He took greenbacks from the madams of Cholon to insure the off-limits orders on their brothels were unenforced. The first thing Olszewski did was look at Goetzler's small hands and thin wrists.

"For Christ's sake, sir, get a Rolex," he said. "No gook will listen to a second lieutenant with a PX Timex."

They busted AWOL draftees from the First Infantry Division, bony rednecks who wouldn't pay the pimps, slow-eyed blacks who killed their buddies over whores. There were explosions, bombs in restaurants, cafés, and go-go bars, the jagged pieces of brick and glass killing the squatting peddlers in from the countryside to sell mangoes and orchids from rice baskets. Sometimes, they trapped the VC bombers in the sewers, and Goetzler and Olszewski watched from the jeep while their men threw grenades into the open manholes like pitchers on the mound.

They pulled the pins, these young MPs in starched jungle fatigues, then did a fast wind-up, laughing and wagging their tongues. Fire in the hole, they yelled. Nobody took cover. After the explosion, the water sprayed up brown and foamy and soaked their legs.

Olszewski held the wheel and kept his foot on the clutch and chewed a Swisher Sweet. Goddammit, Cianci, he said.

The sergeant would stop the jeep suddenly and the tires would lock and they'd slide on the wet streets. Goetzler's neck always jerked and his glasses went spinning into the sunlight. He grabbed after them and got handfuls of humid air. The grayed sergeant just slapped his back. The fucking job, he said. The second week, Goetzler bought an idiot strap at the PX, but the lenses still fogged and he saw Saigon as if through a wet window. He spent his whole tour trying to see correctly, discern the true distances, though it didn't matter because Goetzler and the war became instant friends.

Camille Pajak couldn't get inside his head over here. He loved Vietnam for that alone. There would be no more walks along Belmont Harbor after lectures at DePaul, the lake waves white from the sun, himself tortured by her silence. He didn't care about her great admiration for Emily Dickinson. He was done thinking about her eyes, gray like pond ice, her slender hips, her 36Cs tight inside a sweater, the way her brown hair unraveled in the lake wind when she told him they were the very best of friends. He burned the letters she'd written him in Officer Candidate School about the sparrows in Lincoln Park on the first day of autumn. He'd read them after a day's training, hiding in the dark latrine while the fifty men snored from metal bunks. She sprayed the stationery with Chanel and sent two a week. The cadre sergeants thought it was his cousin being nice. *What could you do with a woman, Goetzler?* But he sat upon the toilet stool and held the paper to his face, knowing her hand touched them. He imagined Paris wet and long nights of lovemaking above rue Cardinal Lemoine where they joined like erotic sculptures while the rain smeared streetlight across the apartment windows. The letters were signed "Always, C," instead of Camille, and he pretended it was a gesture when he knew it was only an opportunity for her to be literary because after graduation she took a job as a legal secretary for Brady, Lunt, and O'Connor.

He was an MP officer now. They said nothing about his small fingers, thick glasses, or how his body would look better on a woman. It was illegal. He bought a nickel-plated Colt .45 with a tricked trigger, the pull lighter than flicking a Zippo. He wore a green cravat under his starched fatigues and smoked a Dunhill pipe filled with Burnham tobacco from Hong Kong. He sported a gold Rolex date timer. For five dollars a week, a lispy Vietnamese kid spit-shined his boots, buffed his MP helmet liner with paste wax, and bleached his white gloves in a bucket. Colonels slapped his back and told him he was the Uniform Code of Military Justice.

Stay squared away, they said, and you own the glory road.

Already, he'd collared a major for beating up a bar girl on Le Loi Street, a square-jawed colonel on Westmoreland's staff who welted her small cheeks with his West Point ring. He pinched a fat lieutenant colonel for selling Johnnie Walker Red from the officers clubs to the bar manager at the Rex Hotel. He escorted the men to Long Binh Jail, cuffed and wide-eyed, their rank meaning nothing.

Mostly, he wanted Camille Pajak to see the girls flock him. Knock him down where he stood. The wispy daughters of South Vietnamese army majors, even the mouthy hookers who claimed their man was a master sergeant in supply, the biggest shot in I Corps, and he was returning next week to take them back to Topeka. New shoes every month and a PX card of their very own. They got naked for a mess hall apple and never pretended to cry about the fate of Virginia Woolf. She put stones in her pockets to drown herself, Camille once said. Stones in her pockets.

That night, after the retirement buffet, Goetzler watched Annie do her lipstick without a mirror. She sat in his chair, her small knees joined and tilted, looking out the high-rise window across Lincoln Park and the gray lake. The money envelope stuck from her Coach bag, six hundred dollars for two hours. He drank his scotch, Laphroaig twelve-year-old, and the whiskey bit over the ice. He could afford this once a week until he was seventy.

Goetzler first saw her on the Web site www.chicagoasian.com. Annie's scanned photo was fuzzy, taken by a hotel room door. She stood with her back to the camera and wore a black thong. He knew she was Vietnamese by her skinny legs. The Thais and Filipinos got more meat as children. Their bones were bigger.

Annie put her phone on the glass table. He asked her last week to come in a yellow *ao dai*. He wanted to reach up through the panels and feel her stomach. He would splay his fingers before drawing them into a slow fist. But she came into his condo wearing a suit and walked across the oak floor in thick boots. The girls always wear what you want, Nick said. You tell me if there's a problem. Goetzler had even turned the heat up because he knew she'd be cold in the yellow silk. Maybe, he thought, it was folded in her bag.

"You need to get changed?" he said.

"I can't wear an *ao dai* for you," she said. "You are not my husband."

Goetzler nodded at her reflection in the glass. Geese flew over the rooftops along Clark Street, a tight V formation.

"The war's old," she said.

Annie lifted her head up and blew like she exhaled smoke.

Her arms were long and thin and the American weight never formed right above her elbows. She'd been looking at his books.

"You have a nice place," she said. "A lot of women would like to sit and look out."

Goetzler put down his drink. The wind lifted the rain up the window. He saw himself reflected in the window, the drops shadowed in his glasses.

"I caught my wife with a supply sergeant over in Germany," he said. "I was a captain."

Annie laughed. Her smooth lipstick cracked when she opened her mouth.

"I bet he was handsome," she said.

"She wanted to drive around Europe in an Alfa Romeo convertible and wear nice sweaters. We did that—right after I got assigned to Berlin. We rented a red one and drove down to Mont Blanc."

The rain held Annie's eyes and he watched them in the window. She pointed at him, her nail long and red.

"Your first anniversary."

"It rained outside Annecy and a tire blew out. We couldn't get the top back up."

"Perfect."

Annie stood and stepped from her boots as if deep in water. She took off her jacket and laid it over the sofa arm. Her shoulders were small, like sticks. She walked over to him and lay down upon the couch with her head against his thigh. He picked up her foot and waited for her to look away from the window. Her heels were white and hard, blanched by hot sand.

"You learned to walk over there," he said.

She was silent.

"You get out on a boat?" he said.

"No. I flew with my wings."

Goetzler watched her stare at the rain before looking out the window, never knowing where the sky and the lake separated.

3

The window blinds muted the streetlight when Mike Spence sat on the bed after his tenth night of Loop traffic control. Susan lay with two cats over one leg, eyeing the bulge where he kept a .38 on his ankle. The snub-nose was backup against the H&K Nine on his hip ever failing. She'd been looking at the concealed pistol for a long time, and he hadn't taken off his uniform. Since Mike went on the job, they spent nights paused in silence rather than fighting about the life he'd just quit.

Susan thought the hidden .38 was ridiculous because Mike waved Sonomas and GMC Jimmys onto the Congress Parkway from State Street.

"You don't know what you're talking about," he'd told her. "I'll need it one day."

After that, Susan stopped seeing him, and looked with un-blinking eyes upon the things he now wore. Mike just went to work.

He touched his wife's ankle, but she didn't move. He left his hand until it made him feel uncomfortable.

"You'll still write?" she said.

"I know what we did for me," he said, "but I don't want to write anymore."

"I didn't choose a cop, Mike."

"It's like the army but I get to come home at night," he said.

"You haven't been a soldier for a long time," she said. "This is just another idea you have of yourself."

"No," he said. "The idea was being a writer."

Susan looked at his light blue Kevlar vest, the same color as his police shirt, then the .38 again. She became a wraith when they talked about this, terrified and near levitating, but he'd stopped feeling bad about it. Susan already knew the answers to her questions, and he believed she didn't have to ask them.

"I can only write about veterans," he said. "And people don't think about veterans the way I know them to end up."

"You can put veterans and their wives in different places," she said. "We've been to Mexico and France. Barcelona. Women will read that."

"I'll never sit alone in a room again," he said. "Todd didn't care about my buddy Dilger and how the lifers ruined him. Todd also has the money to buy books."

"I don't know you," she said.

"I won't keep letting some dream humiliate me," he said.

"We've killed for your dreams," she said.

Mike smiled into his wife's eyes while he undid the Velcro on his Kevlar vest. He was done trying to explain.

"Just like soldiers have for ours," he said.

Susan's eyes wilted, then glassed. She looked from his ankle as if her turning had changed his police blues back into Levi 501s. She then closed her eyes and held them shut. Mike sat for five minutes, stitched inside his wall shadow, and watched her feign sleep. Her eyes never reopened so he stood to raise the blinds.

That night they made love in the hard streetlight, but not to each other. It was what they were doing to forget the problems. They imagined couples from supermarket lines, waitresses in Polish restaurants, women who ran with their dogs. Susan told him things and he told her things, too. They always kept their eyes closed and sometimes he felt her smile while he kissed her. But tonight, among the wind sounds, her lips were straight and coldly wet, and he felt her imagining nothing while he dreamed another man kissing her breasts. Mike tried parting his wife's lips with his tongue, but they wouldn't come open, and the man was licking Susan's stomach when Mike finished. He never let the guy get far.

She touched his arm after he rolled away and looked at him. Her brown eyes once made him angry they were not one person. Now, he did not know when her eyes became only eyes. The wind lifted the curtains and they fell and covered her face before lifting again. He could smell the cold in the wind.

"You're not into it anymore," he said.

"I love you," she said.

She cried and her eyes shook. She lay upon her stomach hugging a pillow.

"It was not a baby," he said.

"They taught me that," she said.

He looked at his dirty uniform on the floor and knew that Susan's eyes were closed without having to see her.

In time, they included visuals into their lovemaking. They used the computer after his traffic shifts, the amateur sites with group sex pictures, the free downloads of home swinger video shot in a Naperville, Illinois, basement, and joined adultfriendfinder.com. They browsed profiles and found many couples like themselves, naked men and women with neither hope nor despair. After they clicked the stranger's thumbnails, they looked a while before smiling and going to bed.

But they didn't own a digital camera and felt uncomfortable with posting pictures, so their ad received no hits. She wanted to keep pretending they swung and Mike felt better. He knew this was a game and that they'd return to normal again. After a few days, they stopped using the computer because the different sites used the same pictures and seeing the people again made them sad. They spent the morning dark quietly while Charlie Rose did a whole week interviewing Wharton School of Business professors about the American economy and neo-conservatism.

One night, Mike and Susan saw an Asian woman in the second-flat window across the street. They'd been watching a *Good Times* marathon on TV Nation when she stood in the lit glass, shirtless with black panties, her body like a half grown cat's. When JJ tried selling an offended Florida on the possibility of a black Jesus, the Asian woman stood so close to the window her breasts pushed flat, and Susan clicked off the television.

"Sit up," she told Mike.

He leaned against the headboard while the Asian woman backed away from the glass. She was drying herself with a towel. Susan sat inside his thighs. Things had gone that fast.

His wife lay back and spread her legs and the streetlight fell across her stomach. She looked out the window at the woman wiping her tiny hips. He kissed Susan's waist.

"Don't touch me," she said. "Your hands are too rough."

Mike and Susan used the woman for a week until the rains came and stripped the leaves from the trees. The lightning slivered without thunder before the thunder clapped alone against the green sky. They touched each other from memories and waited out the storms. Mike imagined the woman kissing his wife, her small hand on Susan's hip. He never asked Susan what she conjured about her, but his wife's lips had stopped feeling cold to him.

When the weather turned east, over Lake Michigan, the woman was leaving at dusk while Susan and Mike read books, separated by the bedroom wall. Every night a different car came for her. There was a black BMW with tinted windows, a blue Jeep Cherokee with clean wheel rims. The cars blocked their view when the woman came from the gangway and drove off quickly. The driver never signaled the turn at the end of the street. They each quietly speculated she was a prostitute.

Three nights later, Susan sat up, wound in the sheet. They'd tried making love, but got stuck while kissing.

"Tell me what I haven't done," she said.

"You've done everything."

"You went to that woman. That is why she left the window."

"I only used her with you."

Mike stared out the window. The rain came steadier, hard as pellets. Susan got up and went to the bathroom. He saw her nakedness in the window and did not look very long. She came out dressed in a T-shirt and shorts with her cell phone.

"No," he said.

"It's too much now," she said.

Susan went to turn the dead bolt. The hallway light shone in the door seams. He grabbed her shoulders and shook her to make her talk. She spat in his face. He hugged her from behind and she screamed without opening her mouth.

"I wanted the baby," he said.

"I didn't want the baby. Not with you. This is not about that."

She kicked at him and pushed back hard and her heels hit his shins. She dug her nails into his arms. When she left him, down the stairs, through one door, then the second, a squall of rain sent sticks spinning against the window. Within a minute, he couldn't touch her anymore.

Mike stayed smug for an hour after his wife disappeared into the city. He sat in the dark and played through Brubeck's *Take Five,* the piano like Pacific blowholes, and let the music help him claim happiness about being done with her. *A writer, Susan? I'm just one of a million dreamers.* He turned the volume until the piano shook the windows, and believed he'd exhaled for the first time in seven years. He saw himself driving coastal roads where rocks broke waves, treeless highways through wheat fields, and wondered why he hadn't pushed this sooner. You give her half the money, he told himself, then imagine a future without her.

We all can't teach retarded kids like you do, he thought.

When the CD reset, the songs started again, but the cool was all gone. The piano now got him above nothing. He shut down the music and grabbed the phone, dialing her cell without watching himself. He sat against the wall, hemmed by shadow lines, and the ringing became voice mail. He hung up, then called right back.

Call me so I don't worry, he said. I won't pick up. Just let me see your number in the caller ID.

Five minutes later, he started leaving the long messages.

Mike Spence sat at the interview table, wondering if it was morning yet. After Detective Ramos had brought him to the station, he put on a dry shirt, but left Mike wet so he could turn up the air conditioner during the interrogation and make him uncomfortable. Mike knew he'd be cleared, but he also knew Susan hadn't been dead very long, killed by a homicidal head injury behind Bell Street, and her murder wouldn't become real until he felt relief about not being a suspect. He was afraid he'd later fall down the precinct house stairs and wail.

The academy taught cops to always sweat the husbands, Mike himself learned, but fat-armed Ramos was freezing him, thinking the increased freon would help Mike realize he'd killed his wife the way Ramos certainly hoped he did. Cops, he knew, loved to bust cops. Mike waited for Ramos to start questioning again, but the detective smoked a Kool and stared at the cinder-block wall.

Mike had seen Susan dead in the alley while the blue police lights strobed through her wet legs. He tried moving, looking away, but the drops wound him, flooding the puddles while they boiled and joined with other puddles. Her sandals had fallen off. One lay by a gangway, the other a few feet from a garbage can. She had crawled to the fence, through the lot lights hooped on the alley, and the rocks stuck in her elbows. When Mike had called, after the eighth message, the patrol cop answered her cell phone and said Mike better come about three alleys east. Just walk for the lights, he'd said.

Ramos dropped a Kool butt into an empty Hawaiian Punch can. His hands stank of grilled onions.

"You are wet, newbie copper," he said. "The cold will sink in."

Mike watched the two cops behind the one-way glass fold their arms alike, then said, "Like I told you. We had a fight and she left. Then the cop answered her phone. You and I got there at the same time. You watched me go down when I saw her dead."

Ramos sagged where he sat. His love handle hung over the Glock Nine on his belt.

"You didn't follow her out with that baseball bat behind your door?" he said.

"Test the bat."

"They've been on your computer, newbie. You direct traffic

in the South Loop, then go home and get into some sick shit. Only she isn't into it like you are."

"It never left the computer."

"I know you smack the shit out of her," Ramos said. "It's your thing. The neighbor heard you arguing about the abortion. You're a fucking asshole."

"No," Mike said. The puddle mud had dried cold on his legs.

"The neighbor hears you fighting all the time," Ramos said. "He told us he warned you."

"I've never hit her."

"We saw where you've kicked the walls."

"The walls aren't my wife."

"I bet you make her blow your buddy?"

"Who?"

"You stand in the room and watch. You whip your skippy in the shadows."

"I want a lawyer."

"You've got something you don't want me to know, newbie."

"I told you."

"You're mad because she likes it with your buddy and you beat her. She tells you he's sweeter and slower. You get off by tearing her up. That's how you fuck?"

"No."

"Rocks off, right? I bet you bring home hookers and make her watch them give you a blow job."

"We had a fight and she left. Then the cop answered her phone."

"No, newbie. You accuse her of loving your buddy, right? You smack her with open hands, but get bored, so you close your fist. You make her cheekbones powder. You chase her outside and kill her in the rain. Did your knees get weak before you came?"

"She was killed and nothing was taken. This is a gang initiation."

"Your neighbor says she teaches retarded kids," Ramos said. "Gangbangers have goofy crack babies. Why would they kill their baby-sitter?"

"I saw her dead when you did," Mike said.

4

In the darkness, in the rainy wind, Annie lay the yoga book on the hardwood floor. She put chair legs over the page corners to keep them flat, and the tall white model looked up at her, even though her eyes were calmly closed, her hands pulling her feet into the bound lotus.

She wanted the book ready, set to a new page of postures, before the cop across the street came from his three-flat. He ran this time every night, rigid like a soldier, his crooked elbows swinging no more than nine inches back. She loved watching his hard legs in the loose shorts he wore, his thigh muscles definite in the streetlight. She'd assume the yoga postures when he was running, always for an hour, his pace faster when he ran back along the row of tightly parked cars, a white towel around his neck. He was a tall man, the one left who never walked a golden retriever, or wore a blue Michigan sweatshirt with the gold lettering cracked from the dryer. He'd hate them, like she did, for thinking life was a cruise through Napa Valley. He ran the alleys, his socks dirty from the puddle water, looking at his watch and trying to make a mile in the last six minutes.

Annie saw the cop in uniform one time. She guessed him a quiet man and he wouldn't want people to know that he was the police. He'd hate the men he worked with, the red-faced guys who rolled the neighborhoods in squad cars, looking for a place to park and watch DVDs on the portable player.

At night, she'd stand in the window, holding her bra in her hands. She tried lighting enough candles for him to notice her topless if he was looking out. I'll stand here for a week, and he'll come running across the street like a dog after birds. But he never crossed Claremont and his shaded window remained dimlit from television. She did keep standing in the window, hoping he watched her back, but understood that this cop never looked at her window when he walked off his run.

There'd been a woman in his apartment nights. Annie once saw her white back in their bedroom TV light. Sometimes she caught the woman looking at her through the dropped blinds because the streetlight lit them and silhouetted her body. But Annie never saw her face. The cop ran to hide from his wife and worked afternoons because it kept his time with her down to a nightly hour. They were not lovers, but two people committed to seeing through an old idea. Annie could tell by the way she lived inside their bedroom when he wasn't home. After Annie stopped working nights, the woman was not there anymore.

Tonight, the cop did not run. She watched with her face so close to the window she smogged the glass with her breath. There was only the dark three-flat where he lived, the small rain leaning through the streetlight. She sat on the floor, studying the Gomukhasana, the cow-face pose. She assumed the position, like the model, a tall white woman who never looked at the camera. The rain cast rolling shadows over the picture. She sat and crossed her legs and bent her knees, her hands joined behind the back, the one elbow pointed up, the other down. *Gomukhasana opens the shoulders and chest to deepen the breath. Emotionally, feelings of melancholy disappear and the blood flow to the heart activates the heart chakra and energy is subtly released.* She read the caption four times, her tight leg muscles flaring to numbness. She squinted her eyes in the grainy light, dragging them slowly across the words twice more, then recrossed her legs. She stretched until her hips throbbed, waiting to feel it vanish.

Annie was five when she hid by the bridge outside Vinh Dinh, stooping in the elephant grass, waiting for a boat with her father and three new uncles. The men shared cigarettes in the white sunlight because the heat dissolved the smoke. Their eyes were squinted and they looked over their shoulders for the brown-shirted police who walked the beach and shot at the boats. She never saw these police, but the uncles said they were close, and pointed at the wood from the wrecked boats.

"We knew each other as boys," her father said of the men. "But when you meet them, you must pretend you can't speak."

She decided she'd act like Huong, her retarded cousin, a girl whose mouth hung open.

Last night, Annie first saw the uncles walking from the pine trees after the rain. Her feet sank coolly into the needles while the moon struck the wet branches. She remembered Huong and made her eyes very wide, letting the smear of the rain take her. She made herself float. But Huong couldn't see their sunburned tattoos, the eagles of the Saigon army. She'd stare and let the stray drops fall inside her eyes. Huong never blinked.

"She's not right," her father told the uncles. "I grab her, she can't make noise."

[35]

He took her arm and shook her. She let her eyes roll up in her head, like Huong did. She kept her lips tight.

The uncles passed a cigarette. But in the darkness, in the dripping pines, they did it behind cupped hands. Their wet faces flared orange when they smoked.

"Why did you bring her?" the toothless uncle said.

Her father took out a length of rope, the one he used for tying his rucksack. He looked hard at the uncle and wound it around her neck.

"If she makes noise," he said.

The men took turns with a cigarette. They held the smoke until none came out.

"The communists won long ago," the toothless uncle said.

"You've seen me use the rope."

"But not for a long time."

The man with the boat never showed yesterday, but her father told the men he'd come today. They watched the sea and the sky, their eyes glowing white from the sun. Her father smiled like these men were his brothers, but the new uncles just passed rice to her father and he gave it to her. One uncle, a tall man without side teeth, rolled the rice into sticky balls. She always could taste his hand.

The sand here burned her feet. She wanted to tell her father that the blisters from last night were wet, and they made colors in the sand. Like yesterday, she thought of her cats lying around her head, back in Hue, their noses wet against their curled tails. Her mother always grabbed the cats, one by one, and threw them to the floor. Le Thuy, she said. They'll suck out your breath. If she could tell her father anything, it would be to change that memory.

When grass shucks bent from the wind, they didn't close back when the breeze died. Suddenly, a soldier was holding a pistol with a string between it and his belt. He wore a dirty khaki shirt, stiff from having been sweat through and dried by the heat. His eyes were soft and brown and she smiled when she saw herself twinned in them.

Huong only sees the sky. She never follows birds.

She wanted to touch the soldier's eyes, reach over and put her finger upon their wet, then touch her own. They'd be nice to see cats with. If she found some, maybe curled under the bridge in the shadow cool, she'd use the wet from his eyes to keep her from blinking. She could stare at the cats until the sampans sailed off the river and the boatmen's dogs stopped barking at the moon.

The soldier raised a pistol. He shot her toothless uncle in the nose, and he fell into his shadow made jagged by the grass roots. The soldier's eyes shook when the earless uncle stabbed him in the neck. He slid off the uncle's chest before he fell into his shadow.

She squatted and smiled and put out her finger to touch his eye. She may find cats when she didn't have to play Huong. She thought cats lived under the bridge and each had a rice basket with a white sheet. Her father might let her look if the boat didn't come. Then she saw the uncle pointing at the bent grass. He was laughing. He wanted to know if her father brought his rope when he ran away. He slapped the knife blade against his thigh.

She was still Huong and her father was looking for the cats so he'd know where to take her later. He might tell her that gray cats were kicked out of the sky because they fell asleep. She wouldn't ask him why. She already knew that gray cats were lazy and didn't do their job of licking the darkness from the clouds. That's why it rained all the time in Hue.

Annie did in-calls for the agency on Friday afternoons. Nick got a room downtown and sent the dates over. They were nervous guys dressed in business casual, khakis and a printed golf shirt. None wore their watches. She laughed when they patted their pockets, their chubby faces panicked, thinking they lost their wallets. You left it at the office with your watch, she'd tell them. She watched them get naked because a cop wouldn't undress, then took the envelope with the money, the six hundred dollars an hour she split with the agency. You go to the bathroom and count it, Nick said. That's the first thing you do.

But that was done for the day.

She sat on the hotel bed, thighs crossed, and waited for the driver. He would call her when he was crossing Michigan Avenue in this rain. She held her cell phone and waited for the fast ring, the blue flash in her hand, hoping Sageer was driving her home. He smelled like Brut soap on a rope and gave her lone roses from 7-Eleven that she carried to her stoop and dropped in the leaves the wind drifted against the porch. But he kept quiet when Bobby never shut up. He drove a blue Grand Cherokee and pointed out the features. The seat memory is here, Bobby told her. There's the gauge for miles per gallon. He'd get out and help her from the car and then touch the small of her back, eyeing her over his glasses. He led her to her door, then brushed his gray hair over a bald spot. The wind always undid it, and the rain made the thin hairs go flat on his scalp.

Her last date of the afternoon had been a talker. She first saw him through the door chain, his thick eyes in the links.

"You're beautiful," he'd said.

Yes, she knew. A twirler.

She closed the room door, undid the chain, then opened it. He was a Gap ad for bloated guys and wore a blue starched oxford.

After he gave her the envelope, he didn't know what to do with his hands, so he pocketed them. The six hundred dollars was in twenties and tens, like he'd been saving for a few months. She pictured his wife putting Starbucks on Visa, paying eighteen percent for mocha lattes and wild berry scones. He went once, a lone cup of coffee in the business, and then lay there touching her, just staring and touching.

"This is worth it," he'd said. "I do it every quarter. And, so you know, we don't pay for sex, we pay for your silence."

She watched the clock on the nightstand, a minute before three. He was nodding to himself, a smile like a slot machine winner, when the hour was up. She stood and his hand hit air trying to touch her.

Right now, the driver was late. Bobby, she thought. He was dumb enough to take Lake Shore Drive off Belmont in the late afternoon. She stared hard at the paintings framed above the headboards. Sailboats were big. The Days Inn Lincoln Park had them tendered in a harbor, the masts bare. The Best Western River North had the boats at sea with sails full of wind. But here, the Motel 6 on Ontario, she couldn't remember the painting when she looked away.

5

In the locker room, Murphy poured water on the sauna rocks while Goetzler felt his *Tribune* pages wilt. They watched the steam rise, but Goetzler a little harder than Murphy, almost like he was aiming a .45. He'd phoned for Annie that afternoon, but Nick told him she was booked through the week, and he'd call if that changed. Goetzler kept his cell phone in the sauna when he knew nobody canceled with her.

Chuck Murphy stayed lean from his constant running on the health club's indoor track. Goetzler just sat in the sauna. Murphy was a boss public defender for Cook County and worked class-three narcotics cases to pay for his daughter's M.Ed., while Goetzler was a divorced corporate man without children or alimony.

Murphy would tell Goetzler he was worried about the mortgage on his cabin in Lake Tomahawk, Wisconsin, and how he was afraid the priests at DePaul University might get everything.

Goetzler only nodded and sweat.

Before law school, Murphy had roomed with Oliver North during USMC Officer Basic School before they'd each led a platoon of marine infantry in Quang Tri, the year after the 1968 Tet

Offensive. Murphy thought North was a dedicated man, but it was good the Marine Corps had forced North into retirement. Even during Iran Contra, he never told Goetzler anything more.

Goetzler had known Murphy since he resigned his military police commission in 1975, himself still a captain, but then with Army Criminal Investigative Division in Bamberg, West Germany, where his glasses never fogged. Goetzler had gotten a general's son relieved when he discovered a heroin ring in the boy's mechanized infantry company, led by two draftee Gangster Disciples from the West Side of Chicago, and the general had Goetzler passed over for major the third time. But Goetzler only talked to Murphy in the sauna and knew of his life and family from the stories he told. Goetzler did like him, and thought Chuck Murphy a patriot even though he joined Vietnam Veterans Against the War upon returning from Quang Tri Province in 1970, and believed he saw atrocities when, as Goetzler told him, he was only fighting guerrillas and they required such methods.

The third time they'd ever pitched water on the sauna rocks, Murphy looked at Goetzler, whose detective-captain-uncle, Kerm Goetzler, had just made him a Chicago cop, a job he'd hold for two years. Army majors live in duplexes, Uncle Kerm had told Goetzler, looking at his nephew's silver Rolex, police sergeants have a bungalow and two three-flats.

Murphy shook his head like a trial lawyer. Goetzler had been talking about how America quit in Vietnam and the United States Government had sold every veteran down the river. Our legacy, he told Murphy, remains a sad joke because we didn't guard it like the World War II veterans did.

"I wasn't going to ask a man to be the last person to die for a lie in Vietnam," Murphy borrowed. "That's not the legacy I wanted."

Goetzler tried his best Robert Mitchum from behind his steamed glasses, still believing Chuck Murphy was dumb enough to believe his cop routine.

"I was a professional soldier, Chuck," he said. "You were a reserve officer. I believe I could serve in any army. It wouldn't matter."

Murphy laughed at him with a closed mouth.

"You're a cop, now," he said. "You were a cop then. And I've cross-examined enough cops to know they are too smart to be soldiers."

"Why is that?"

"Because soldiers are too dumb to be cops. That's how you MPs get so lucky. What match is a drunk grunt when you're shaking down a whorehouse?"

Today, Goetzler had Murphy because he couldn't get Annie. He was glad he could always find him, but as they grew older, Murphy reminded Goetzler of losing because so often he sat in this sauna by default. You can't work your bullshit on me, Murphy would tell him. I've seen you naked more times than I have my Mary Therese.

Murphy pitched the last cup of water on the rocks, then took the steam with his face. Goetzler laughed at him for believing that every afternoon he could sweat the bad things out. Murphy was always kayaking in Lake Superior and Lake Michigan, or running the Lakeview streets, smiling like he could wash most of life away. He'd just put his Lincoln Park town house on the market and was retiring from the public defender's office. He wanted to pay off the cabin and the priests inside twenty-four hours, then grow old paddling in Wisconsin until he had a heart attack and drowned. Goetzler knew he'd be in Chicago only another two months.

"So you live your whole life to go die by a Wisconsin lake," Goetzler said.

Murphy sat smiling in a towel.

"You are a decorated marine and successful civil servant and you want to check out beside a north wood pond. A lifetime of bad-mouthing your country should come to more than that."

"No," he said. "When I start feeling chest pains over eighty, I'm taking a birch kayak into Lake Superior. It beats dying in hot paddy mud or the hot sand."

"At least the men in the mud and the sand go fighting. They will never know the feeling of being defined by men who were not there."

"I know you don't think that way," he said.

"They died believing an idea of themselves. That's the best way to go."

"There's a cabin for sale right next to mine," Murphy said. "We could sit in my sauna and forget we're not the Greatest Generation. We'll have a time, Donny. We'll let everything fall away."

"Nothing falls away."

"You've watched too many movies."

"You galloped at too many windmills," Goetzler said.

He wanted to tell his friend how he censored himself these years to keep him from seeing inside, but Murphy would just laugh, and say, you cops always try getting something on the world by pretending to kill your hearts. Instead, Goetzler sat quietly and watched Murphy squeeze sweat from his bicep pores, knowing there were two more months until Murphy vanished like a dead Indian, or an Irishman gone to America. After he moved north, there'd be a lot of silence, and Goetzler tried not thinking about it.

————

After Vietnam, Goetzler busted a general's son in Bamberg, West Germany, Captain Douglas Rogers Junior, a sweaty-lipped company commander in Second Armored, West Point 1969. Surveillance found the captain had two black NCOs in his company with Vietnam tours dealing heroin they got from Barcelona by way of Tunis. They supplied Second Armored with smack and drove new Mercedes-Benzes. Then, black soldiers with Asia time started disappearing, six AWOLS in two weeks, and Goetzler saw a stateside gang connection: Chicago Vice Lords and Gangster Disciples were coming to Germany instead of Southeast Asia in 1974 and had freedom to operate. The AWOL soldiers all came from Inglewood, Sixty-third and Cottage Grove where the night hung dark between broken streetlights. The six were Vice Lords, loud kids from the South Side beaches. They were killed over business, shot and dumped in the muddy Rhine with cinder blocks chained to their ankles, but the last two were just dropped in the brown water, and the West German police found them washed up against a bridge pier west of Düsseldorf.

Goetzler wore a dark suit now, a Strafford from London, the uniform of Army Criminal Investigations. He saluted no one. He walked into the offices of captains and lieutenant colonels all over Second Armored, hung his wet trench coat over chair backs, and asked them what they planned to do about the drug problems in their units. The officers always sweated, thin beads between the nose and the upper lip. They pulled at West Point rings and looked at pictures of their wives upon the metal desks, small, mean women, former beauty queens from South Carolina teaching colleges. In the beginning, Goetzler never minded how the officers clubs paused when he walked inside. Men turned their backs and resumed their conversations in low tones. One time, an old transportation colonel asked him how he expected to plot a career when his job was to make people look bad. I have my orders, Goetzler said.

But already the stories about Goetzler's wife preceded him like a bad smell. The MPs found her kissing Sergeant Nick Camarda's hairy stomach in Goetzler's own BMW one night along the back fence of the supply depot in West Berlin. He was a skinny guy with hair on his knuckles who tore the filters off Kools before he smoked them. Officers loved to laugh at bad ones like this. I know this CID guy, a captain with ten years, they'd say. They caught his wife with a wop supply sergeant from II Corps. The golf ball through the garden hose joke circulated all over II Corps, and now the officers smiled at him when he walked into the club for dinner. Goetzler wished he could laugh with them, grin ear to ear like he'd been short-sheeted in the barracks.

His wife had been a teller at LaSalle Bank in Chicago before the wedding. He only married her so the army wouldn't think he was gay. She was part man and she used her body like a tough cop might, bullying with a thin waist and fleshy hips, even believing her shoulders square and thick. She imagined them cruising Europe in sleek rental cars, convertibles, like Dustin Hoffman had in *The Graduate*. The sun had to be a certain way in the mirror, low to the ground, and the sky pink and blue and white where the white sunlight hazed along the horizon. She made him pay for not making that happen. I have my needs, she said.

Goetzler got back-channel word from Third Army in Frankfurt to solve the heroin problem. But Second Armored, "hell on wheels through the hedgerows," never admitted it went crazy with dope after 1970. Men were stoned at rifle ranges and shot out the target stakes, laughing with open mouths. They mainlined heroin before inspections and stared at the officers with wide, happy eyes.

The soldiers dropped blotter acid sent from the states in paper-back novels and listened to Pink Floyd on reel to reel tape decks in dark barracks' rooms lit by black lights and lava lamps. Their walls were covered with velveteen artwork: Hendrix with the white Stratocaster, the cover of *Led Zeppelin I*, toothy tigers jumping from jungles. Goetzler made the case by searching Staff Sergeants Tyrone Wills's and Anthony Green's red Mercedes-Benzes. The heroin was in their trunks like an extra tire jack, and Goetzler sent them to Leavenworth for life. The general's son was relieved of command and sent stateside to be a range officer at Fort Benning's Infantry School.

The captain's father was Major General Douglas Rogers Senior, West Point 1942, now G3-Operations at Third Army, a gaunt man with prizefighter's eyes who won the Distinguished Service Cross at Monte Casino, and married a woman he first glanced in a Tuscan hill town while retreating from the Germans in late 1943. He came back after the war and found her in a ruined café, pouring an old man espresso and kicking stray dogs away from the table with dirty bare feet. She claimed she remembered Rogers, his glance through the sideways rain while German artillery hit the river, and married him the day the paperwork cleared headquarters. The army press repeated the story in post newspapers whenever the old man got a new assignment. There were before and after pictures. She had wide hips, dark eyes, a perfect 36C, and looked at him the way a hungry person does a waiter.

Rogers sat in officers clubs with the few classmates that hadn't retired, thin men who'd went gray on their thirty-fifth birthdays. He wasn't going to let some draftee frag his son. He got him a job on Creighton Abram's Saigon staff in late 1972. He lived near the embassy, along Tu Ten Street. Goetzler figured the captain had a snapshot of him and his father having dinner on the rooftop of the Rex Hotel. There were no women in *ao dai,* poised like cats on the officers' laps. The men ate steak and looked at their watches.

The general had an infantry division there late in the war and claimed he led junkies, pimps, and thieves into Cambodia. I have to be honest, he said. I was scared of the enlisted. The rumor went that Doug Rogers told a reporter that under the condition of anonymity. Goetzler knew three officers were killed by fragging in his division, hit during firefights with hand grenades at very close range, and two had died in Cambodia.

He summoned Goetzler to Third Army headquarters. He sent a courier down to Bamberg, some starched PFC in a Department of Defense Ford. The orders were specific. Report in uniform, 1300 hours.

The general's face was lean, his cheekbones definite. He sat behind his desk with his hands behind his head, his legs crossed at the knee. He looked at Goetzler as if watching TV from a couch. The red flag with his two white stars hung from a wooden pole in the corner. The office was nice, an executive's desk, a padded leather swivel chair, but the window looked upon the headquarters' parking lot and the general's own reserved space. Goetzler had expected something different, maybe a few more potted plants, a wet bar stocked with package store bourbon, but it was a room in a big building, like one square in an ice cube tray.

Rogers kept Goetzler at attention, locked up in his green uniform. The sweat ran down his back. His shaving cuts burned.

"My boy is taking an assignment in the South Carolina National Guard," the general said. "He got a job in a bank, Goetzler. Charleston First National. He'll sign off on car loans to start."

The general's eyes were smug but terrified. His two stars hadn't helped his son. The army today was like the HMS *Bounty* after the crew sent Bly off in the rowboat. Goetzler could see the general never imagined Vietnam would cause all of this.

"Can you understand the humiliation?" he said.

The general waved Goetzler quiet before he spoke.

"He went to West Point, Captain Goetzler. Twenty-first in his class. You think he fooled with dope."

"No, sir."

"Wrong place, wrong time about my boy. Wouldn't you think?"

"I'd guess, sir."

"You think his wife would fornicate with the enlisted?"

"No, sir."

"By the way, Captain, was your ex-wife from the North?"

"Yessir."

"Those women are not suited to this life. But my daughter-in-law's father was a colonel, Captain. From Mobile. This is our home."

"The war changed the army, sir."

"There hasn't been a war in thirty years."

"I mean Vietnam, sir."

"That was for draftees and OCS lieutenants. It's over now and time for the regular army to reflect on its true procurement goals."

Goetzler felt weak all the way down.

"So, you think you'll go into banking, Captain Goetzler. Maybe real estate? I think selling Fords might be a worthwhile pursuit. Good solid cars, Captain Goetzler. I'll write you a letter of reference. That would be my absolute pleasure."

The general nodded his head to dismiss him. The starched

PFC courier opened the door after he pressed a button by his phone. Goetzler imagined his legs going like a closing telescope while he saluted.

After Goetzler set his cell ringer to vibrate, he dropped the phone in his pocket, still waiting for some guy to cancel with Annie. He walked the nursing home hallway and looked for the door with Uncle Kerm's name written on a piece of masking tape. Kermit Goetzler was dying, but he made eighty-five drinking vodka martinis on the rocks and smoking Camel filters, and the heart problems only started six months ago. The bachelor-detective-captain kept his habits until the end.

Goetzler took his time down the hallway, knowing a faster pace would give Uncle Kerm more time to proclaim how he beat them all. He looked in rooms where men and women lay in Christmas-gift sweat suits looking out the windows, then watched his shoes hit the shiny tiles, wishing his phone would vibrate.

Uncle Kerm finished his working life tougher than Goetzler and his father had. He was a detective captain when he retired with ten three-flats and a thirty-five-footer he rarely sailed in Belmont Harbor. Goetzler's father played the guitar, watched TV baseball, and sent his mother to the grocery store with a pull cart and pension money from the tool and die makers local 165. They seemed only brothers by law. Goetzler's father never forgave Kerm for flying a Mustang against Stukas on the Italian Front after his father got discharged from the navy for shitting his pants in boot camp, a problem his father corrected by forcing Goetzler to catch balls and shoot pheasant without his thick glasses. Kerm neither cared if his brother ever forgot messing himself in the chow line, nor how he took the permanent humiliation out on his kid by making him try catching baseballs. Kerm was a tall man with a smooth face and so darkly handsome the guys in his detective squad called him the wop even though he was German. Anytime, he could finish a Camel and check his silver oyster Rolex and feel that his hands weren't calloused from working a lathe. Uncle Kerm also knew his brother never smelled his wife on him, and Goetzler figured it was a big gag these years.

In the mornings, Goetzler's mother would wait upstairs for Kerm, naked beneath the two white towels, and stare out the window. She'd think her son was gone, learning to play CYO dodge ball without his glasses because his father took them to Finkel and Sons and kept them locked in his toolbox. She was a beautiful woman who watched the wind blow tree limbs all day, and after turning seventy, started knitting clothes for her cats.

But Goetzler never left the bungalow on Logan Boulevard. He'd hide in the basement and dream himself a U-boat commander silent among British merchant ships, the water pipe his periscope. He even made a captain's hat from paper and staples, drawing the Kriegsmarine eagle with a pen. His imagined men wore beards, but he was clean-shaven.

The first time Kerm let himself in the back door, Goetzler was ready to fire a torpedo at an American destroyer in the North Sea. The ship lifted between the swells while the rain drove hard. Then Goetzler heard the wind take the screen door, and he turned from the drain pipe, wearing his paper hat, the bill blackened by crayon.

Uncle Kerm was combing his hair in the foyer while the rain blew through the screen and rolled off his shoes. He looked at Goetzler, shaking the water off the comb, and lit a Camel with his

Air Corps Zippo. He pointed at his hat with the cigarette, the smoke rising like kite string. A nickel-plated .45 hung beneath his wet armpit.

"I'll get you a real one of those," he said. "There's Nazi leftovers in basements all over the city. I know a couple of guys."

Goetzler squinted to see Kerm while he removed his jacket and slung it over his arm. His eyes were still focusing when his uncle turned on a heel and went upstairs to his mother, his smoking nearly sounding like laughter. But the next time Kerm used his key, he carried a Kriegsmarine Hauptmann's hat in a bag, and gave Goetzler a surplus Iron Cross, 3d Class besides. After the first summer, Goetzler had a Luftwaffe gas mask, a Waffen SS helmet, and a dummy potato-masher grenade.

In the nursing home, his uncle rented the only carpeted private room on the east wing. His window looked over Lake Michigan and he could bribe the nurses with chocolate. They let him play his Ramsey Lewis CDs until midnight, and gave him two 10-milligram Xanaxes a week if he brought them Godiva.

After Kerm had turned eighty, his eyes went black, dark as shoes, but they still stared long and unblinking. When he'd made captain at fifty, the guys continued asking him to buy their cars because Kerm's eyes made the salesman's intestines bloat from nervous fear during the test drive. You know I want to buy a car today, he'd say. He got the best price out of people. But the guys stopped calling him the wop, even though he still combed his hair straight back at hotel bars and lit his cigarettes with a platinum Zippo. It was time. He was a captain now. He kept a peroxide blonde in a studio on Clark Street, and she even quit her job cashing checks at LaSalle Bank. I never got to spend the night, he'd say.

When Goetzler walked into the room, Uncle Kerm was sitting in bed watching Bloomberg on a thirty-six-inch Sony, his laptop open to Ameritrade. His hair had gone white, but remained thick and toniced. He wore a heavy cotton robe, a gold oyster Rolex, Grey Flannel by Geoffrey Beene, and played with his Air Corps Zippo even though he'd quit smoking. Goetzler waited while Uncle Kerm watched the numbers roll past, the Dow always slower than the NASDAQ.

"Goddamned Kmart," he said to Goetzler. "They invented the idea and lost everything. I know they give retired army officers jobs. But that's like putting cops in charge of passing out the dole. Lifers are lazy thieves at heart, Donny."

"I sent lots of them to Leavenworth," Goetzler said. "The supply sergeants couldn't stop stealing, and the mess sergeants were dumb enough to sell mess hall pork chops on the local market."

Kerm laughed and waited for the afternoon bell at the New York Stock Exchange before turning away from the television. Goetzler saw his uncle's Rita Hayworth screensaver, the famous silk sheets pose. The old man was looking out at the lake.

"You could have retired like I did," Kerm said. "A boat and money for broads. All the pollocks and micks kissing your police captain ass."

"I did fine with Weber."

"You asked contractors if they read the catalog," Kerm said. "And the cops never would have clipped you like the suits did. I told you those boys have no code."

Goetzler had forgotten the chocolates for the nurses. If he kept quiet, his uncle would talk until he forgot last week's request. Though, he never wanted to stop being a cop or a soldier. When he came home from Germany, he decided that if the army hadn't let him remain a professional soldier, the Chicago police department would. But he'd shot a kid heroin dealer in the knee, firing quickly, like the kid was Saigon VC, and Internal Affairs determined the young man was unarmed and carrying two nickels of heroin. Mike Rosen, the criminal defense lawyer representing the kid, forced the department to settle for sixty thousand dollars and require Goetzler to attend Vietnam Veterans group therapy if he wanted his badge. Kerm tried fixing things, but failed since Rosen got a City News reporter interested in tracking Goetzler's requirement, and Kerm never would admit the limits of his power. The department was adamant and Goetzler left the job after two years as a flatfoot. That group would've been like talking to Chuck Murphy, Kerm finally said. They'd have called you on your bullshit.

His uncle flipped the channel from Bloomberg to Telamundo, the Spanish cable station. He watched the Mexican girls in neon thongs play beach volleyball in off-season Cancún, keeping the volume muted because he hated the music.

"You were too pissed off at the guys who didn't go to Vietnam. It screwed you out of being a police captain."

"I had a good career at Weber."

"They iced you, Donny. If you'd stayed on the job, you'd be an area commander by now. You had my friends until you got squirrelly about going to the VA shrink. That lawyer wanted you fired or he'd sue in federal court. My friends stood up and argued him down."

"I wasn't sitting in that group. I did nothing wrong in Vietnam."

"Listen to me," Kerm said. "The group was a goddamned hoop. Nobody in the department understands Vietnam enough to give a shit—even the guys who were there."

Goetzler was silent.

"You come home from a war," Kerm said. "You get laid for

a month, then you forget about it. You can't punish the lucky guys who stayed behind. They wouldn't learn from a beating anyway."

Goetzler watched the TV screen reflected in the window. The volleyball players were blurry against the lake. He was long done telling his uncle why he wouldn't go to the group. He'd used all the arguments. Those groups, Goetzler might say, contain humiliated men who would be in a group even if they never saw the Republic of South Vietnam. It was useless. For Kerm, war was something you got over by living well. He'd wave Goetzler away with a lit Camel, then say, "The damn group was just a hoop, Donny."

6

It turned hot the month after Susan died. The wind quit for a week and the car exhaust lingered, blurring the Loop lights. The department forced Mike into bereavement leave, and he spent the time at his mother-in-law's clapboard house after they'd spread Susan's ashes in a creek that ran between an apple orchard and a cornfield. It was just them, Mike and the widow afraid to walk to Wal-Mart by herself. For three days, she talked to him factually and never looked into his eyes. A kid would have made Suzy-Q get over her temper. Her dad was smart enough to know that.

But his mother-in-law was gone now, like his wife, and he stood nights at State and Congress, directing traffic in a surgical mask against the car exhaust. He waved some lanes to turn. He held others still with his raised palm. When his underarms became wet, his shaving cuts burned, and he hoped he wouldn't start coughing from the smog. It forced his eyes closed and the intersection went to pieces.

He always began his shift trying to slow down the Range Rovers. They turned fast and sharply so they'd go over on two wheels. His sergeant told him he'd seen three flip this past year.

Mike stopped them with his white gloves and handed young millionaires hundred-dollar tickets. They condescended politeness and called the hundred dollars meter change. He was a city employee to them, some dumb guy who picked the gun over money.

After dinner break, Mike didn't care about enforcing as much, and let the Range Rover guys have their ideas of themselves. The nights went better when he finally settled. He'd try spending the last hours looking for a directing rhythm that faded his memories about wanting to push a button and make Susan disappear when things first went bad between them. He never found the thoughtless rote. When the traffic signals became routine, his mind went racing. The tactical squad was formed in the break room when Mike Spence walked past the Coke machine. He'd gotten reassigned to gang crimes when the department decided he'd not killed his wife, and discovered he'd jumped into Panama with the 82d Airborne Division. Now, he was in civilian clothes, a gun and cuffs on his belt, ready to roll through neighborhoods and shake down teenagers selling grass too close to Starbucks. He was vaguely happy. This duty beat standing and remembering.

The tactical squad was chubby, thick-shouldered guys with the same bulletproof vests and pistols that cost an even grand. Nobody raised his eyes and gave Mike the new guy haze, the asshole grins, the gum chewed openmouthed. They leaned against the wall and held leather jackets and dozed chin to chest, or sat on the table with their feet on chairs and dipped Snickers bars into Dunkin' Donuts coffee. He expected the paratroopers he served with fifteen years ago, the way Corporal Mickey McDowell eyed him cold and swore in Southy brogue that they better stick a fork in this cherry's ass because he looked done. He'd stoned up his face, ready to take the tac squad's eyes, but there were no whore winks or hard stares. They sat quietly while the rain hit the windows, a cold and blowing rain, thankful they never wrote traffic tickets during blizzards. Mike stood by the Coke machine and drank his coffee.

Sergeant Kenjuan Mills walked through the door but didn't cross the room. He wore baggy jeans showing Calvin Klein boxers and his Air Jordans were white like he was carried over the puddles. The oldest guy in a ghetto club, Mike thought.

Mills glanced at his Rolex, a gold date timer. He smiled while the watch slid from his leather jacket sleeve.

"Who's up today?" he said. "The whores or the pimps?"

The white guys sitting on the table said nothing. They glanced sidelong and bored while Mills looked at the watch.

"The pimps are always up," one said.

Mills looked at the black and showed his diamond pinkie ring. He put the finger in the air, letting him see.

"You gain ten more pounds, dog, Shylonda won't let you hit that shit."

"All fat ass Tony Soprano does is look and they come."

"You ain't T."

The black smiled and sneezed without covering himself. Mills's nostrils flared before he looked away.

"Goddamn, Avery, cover yourself."

"You see what Tony Soprano gets," the black said.

"Yeah. Russian girls without a leg."

Mills shook off his hands.

"The story today is Hector and James over the car hood," he said. "They've been breaking into garages all over Lakeview. You guys cuff them and make the numbers. Then what happens, Hernandez?"

The Mexican sneered, then spat gum in the garbage can. The white guys looked at the ceiling.

"Your black ass hits the glory road," Hernandez said.

"And what do I get for you?"

Hernandez didn't see Mills, just the wall behind him.

"Plenty of court overtime," he said. "I get lunch at the El Presidente on Twenty-sixth Street and eyefuls of Carmen with the big titties filling baskets with tortilla chips. I never drive the wagon and pick up bloated stiffs from apartments filled with cats and yellow newspapers."

"New man here knows?" Mills said.

Mike drank black machine coffee while Mills eyed his hands. He was standing like a rottweiler.

"New man here wrote a book," he said. "You all know that?"

The white guys didn't look at Mike. They eyed their surplus combat boots and took a breath. The blacks drank the bottoms of their Mountain Dews and waited for the caffeine hit. Mills smiled and showed two gold teeth.

"I read it," he said. "He thought the Jennifers should be standing in line to suck his dick because he watched his buddy get beaten in the army for no reason. And why should Brian pay twenty-five dollars for new man to call him a pussy?"

"He didn't," Mike said.

"I know that," Mills said. "Now you come on the job to write another?"

"No. I just came on the job."

"I'll fix you up with a good war, new man. I'll get you staring off a thousand yards."

Mills smiled and studied Mike and his hands. His cell phones went off, the ringers set the same. He put down a big gulp Hawaiian Punch on the table and took out the phones. He raised one to his ear before the other and grinned wider after each ring. Mike walked over and looked out the window and watched Mills nodding in the glass.

Mike Spence drove through Lakeview in the unmarked Crown Victoria while Hernandez drank his fourth Coke. A landscape of new houses built in six weeks and clapboard wood frames bought last year for tear down and rehabbed gravestones turned condo with sale placards six months old in the rain-dirty windows. There were new streets and curbs and along them tightly parked Audis and Volvo wagons. He turned into the alley and hit the flooded potholes, making the empty bottles roll across the muddy floor mats.

Hernandez had an Indian face with long cheekbones. He'd urinated in a Coke bottle, but dropped it on the floor, and the cap popped off. He sopped the piss with torn pages from the *Sun-Times*. Mike rolled down the window and the rain slanted into his face. The reek wouldn't shake.

"You know what today is?" Hernandez said.

"Yesterday with rain."

Hernandez sat up and chewed gum. He tapped a meringue beat on the dashboard.

"The welfare checks hit Humboldt Park," he said. "All the mommies got a bill in their purse. They're at T.J.Maxx and Marshalls buying panties and bras. They let you watch. They hold it up to themselves and look right at you."

Mike stared out the window, blinking long enough to see black.

"You'd do fine there," Hernandez said. "A big white guy. Shit. They'd be holding up those purple bras and smiling at you."

Mike drove and turned out the alley mouth and passed a fake Irish pub with six-dollar pints. The rain blew sideways over the graystone roofs and wetted the parking tickets on the parked Range Rovers and Saabs and Grand Cherokees. He watched Hernandez flip the visor down, then up.

"You don't know about the mommies?" he said.

"I spent my probation downtown. Traffic control."

"The ones with kids are the best. They got to work harder to keep you."

Mike nodded while the rain slackened.

"Mills is there right now."

"There's next month," Mike said.

Hernandez took out his Newports. He opened another Coke and lit a cigarette off a Zippo engraved with the Marine Corps bulldog.

"No. We'll be out here guarding condos and SUVs."

"Fine with me," Mike said. "I went tac for the overtime."

"Lifer."

"I'll do my twenty, but I'll never go to my knees."

Hernandez smoked and flipped the lighter top up and down.

Mike watched a blond woman push a stroller, walk a golden retriever with drool lines, and drink coffee.

"You remind me of this one white guy," Hernandez said. "Tommy Thiel. He hit Mills. That's why he's got two gold teeth."

"I bet Mills gave back."

"Without a gun?" he said. "Mills just pulled rank."

"Why'd he hit him?"

"Mills told Tommy he was too afraid to get out of the car and make the numbers."

"Then he popped him?"

"Knocked Mills on his ass. He came back two days later with

the gold teeth. Tommy's out at O'Hare on 9/11 detail. He walks around with a radio and checks for unattended bags. Mills made the lieutenants list. Fuck up, move up."

Mike said nothing. He looked at Hernandez and then looked out at the street. The wind blew maple leaves from the trees and they splayed on the wet windshield.

"You got to be careful," Hernandez said.

"There's white guys on the squad."

"Konick and McCaffrey. They just bought two-flats in Jefferson Park. They eat his shit with a spoon."

Mike turned into the alley while the rain bore into the plastic, rat-proof garbage cans. Hernandez watched a small TV he kept between his legs. It was a talk show, heavyset white women were pointing and shouting at a skinny guy who sat onstage with his arms crossed. He glanced over at Mike when the commercials started.

"Tomorrow I'll bring my DVD player," he said. "I'm in Blockbuster Rewards so I get two for one on Wednesdays."

"Sure."

"Maybe they'll make a movie from your book," he said. "I think those are the best movies. What's yours about?"

"Paratroopers from Fort Bragg. We used to drive up to Chapel Hill and crash frat parties and start fights."

"I was in the marines at Lejeune. We did the same thing. This guy Avila had a van with the globe and anchor painted on the sides. We went there and tore the place up."

Mike nodded. The small TV screen glowed against the door. The guys home early from work were pulling black BMWs into their garages. Some walked from the El station at Sheffield, their umbrellas sturdy like their German cars. The autumn dark came fast.

"We used to sweat college boys," Hernandez said.

"I saw you guys do it," Mike said. "I had a girlfriend at UNC."

"We were some shit."

"You were that."

Hernandez was still proud of himself after Mike had turned into the alley.

Past Racine Avenue, Mike saw a skinny black dangling from the cistern of a rehabbed wood frame. He flailed his legs and had lost a shoe. The window was broken and the wind pushed the blinds back into the room. Mike had looked over and there the kid was.

"Keep going," Hernandez said.

Mike drove behind the next garage. He shut down the car and opened the door and stepped into a puddle over his boot toes.

"Call it in," he said.

Mike took out his H&K Nine and walked between the garages. He kept the pistol along his leg. The glass from the window lay upon the patio with the kid's lone high-top. He hung with cushy headphones over his ears and tried getting his footing on the ledge. The cistern pulled away from the roof and went slack and the kid lowered by fast inches. His feet were below the ledge and he flailed his legs and his plastic leg fell off and bounced three times on the wet concrete. His empty sweatpant leg inflated like a windsock. Then the cistern halved and he dropped straight down with a shower of rotten leaves. He hit and fell sideways, his mouth open, his teeth gaped and splayed.

"Motherfucker," he yelled. "Oh, motherfucker."

The kid lay on the ground with his good leg trapped inside his baggy sweats. It was bent back at the knee, his heel wedged against his backside. He strained to look behind him, then looked past Mike, the music still popping from his headphones.

Mike holstered his pistol. The kid slapped the pant leg with open fingers.

"You see my leg?" He talked loudly over the music.

"I don't see your leg," Hernandez said. He'd walked up between the garages and leaned against the fence and lit a cigarette in the rain. He had an easy way about himself, like time was reefer to smoke.

"Shit," the kid said.

"Maybe you can steal a skateboard," Hernandez said. "You could scoot your punk ass around on that."

The kid was still trying to look behind himself. Mike started after the leg where it lay on the concrete and turned the rain. Hernandez looked at him and shook his head.

"Medicaid won't buy you another."

The kid cried badly, his face like breaking glass.

"You make bond tonight," Hernandez said, "you steal a skateboard. Gloves, too. The concrete will fuck up your hands."

A long horn blew from the alley. Hernandez walked past the kid and looked back at Mike.

"Take that," he said.

Mike went off between the garages. The exhaust was thick in the darkness and the rain seemed to fall through it.

The guy stood outside his Range Rover in the rain. He reached through the open door and lay upon the horn. His hair had been gelled, feathered, and wavy until he stepped from the vehicle and into the drops. He was almost tall and very lean from spin classes. His nose came at you.

"You're in front of my garage," he said.

Mike checked his holster snap. Already the black SUVs were lined behind the Range Rover and their headlights showed the rain. These people liked riding up high. He even bet this guy's name was Todd.

"Police business," Mike said. "Back it up."

"Show me how I can do that," he said. "Just tell me how."

Mike smiled and lifted up his hands.

NPR was loud on the Range Rover's door speakers, some story about single mothers in Arkansas convincing Wal-Mart to open in-store day-care centers. I'm a better employee for it, a woman drawled.

"You can't just block alleys," the guy said.

"It's a crime scene," Mike said.

"Is my garage a crime scene?"

Mike saw people after the wipers passed the windshields, just the lone silhouettes of them, glowing green from the dash light. The guy was looking at him.

"I know a lot of city attorneys," he said.

"How'd you get so important?"

The guy's neck went stiff. His lips moved. He was talking himself into something.

"Fuck you," the guy said.

Mike walked across the puddles, breaking the reflected light.

"Fuck you." He smiled dry white teeth. He'd worked himself up to it and now he'd done it twice.

Mike grabbed the guy and bounced him off the door frame until his knees caved. He laid him over the hood and grabbed a handful of hair and slammed his face. One by one, the SUVs were backing down the alley, their tires loud on the pavement.

7

Goetzler sat with his friend for the last time in the sauna, his cell phone wrapped in a towel, and waited for Nick to call him back about Annie. Murphy sold his bungalow before the realtor had put out a sign. In the morning, he was leaving Lakeview, the Volvo-choked corner of Bosworth and Wrightwood, for a lifetime of cold-water kayaking in Lake Tomahawk, Wisconsin. Everything Mary Therese wanted to keep was already up north, he'd said:

Murphy's house was solid, but nothing special. Chicago bungalows were only two-bedroom apartments with an attic and half basement.

He then tried telling Murphy about the cop he'd seen beating a man in the headlights of a Range Rover, but Murphy was too high from getting seven hundred thousand dollars after having bought the place for thirty-five. I was cutting through an alley, Goetzler told him. This cop was hitting a hairsprayed suit, holding his balled collar and giving him jabs.

Murphy was too nature-dreamy to listen.

"The guy must have mouthed the cop," Goetzler said, "but

the cop had the honor to smack him in front of the world. You could tell the guy had never been hit. But he'll never learn that the law is not money."

Murphy talked right over Goetzler.

"I'm trying to understand how the young couple who bought this bungalow for seven hundred thousand could move in with five percent down," he said. "The salary he must have."

"You were a public defender. This guy is a lawyer."

"He's thirty-five and she doesn't work."

"It wasn't like this when you bought here," Goetzler said. "These are different people than the people you know."

"I know people."

"The people a public defender knows."

"You're not going to make me bitter, Donny. You haven't won yet."

"I'm just telling you."

"No. You're wanting flesh and you don't know how to get your pound. Just buy the cabin next to mine and we'll think about other things."

"And eat overcooked steaks in Wisconsin supper clubs?"

"Let's just sweat, Donny."

Goetzler would tell Murphy that the cop was tired of keeping the world fair for men who believed themselves absolutely correct. He serviced them, they humiliated him, and the cop was done with this two-stroke food chain. Aware of the possible price, the fallout from hitting a civilian, this cop took his pound of flesh anyway. But Murphy wouldn't care enough to listen. He'd retired from the public defender's office, the years of hopeless first-degree murder defenses, and only planned to see game wardens toting old .38s until his last sunrise. They sat quietly until Murphy told Goetzler he'd be back next summer and that he'd call him. They parted and agreed to sweat in June. Murphy would stall the cabin owner for a couple months so Goetzler could think about buying.

Later, in the locker room, Goetzler dressed. He used number 346 because it was close to the security mirror and he could watch men's hands in the bubbled glass. Always keep watch of their hands, Kerm told him when he became a flatfoot. The one thing you know for sure is that you don't know what will happen next.

After he got booted from the force, he sat in a windowless room for twenty-five years and ran focus groups of plumbing contractors, the fat sons of the guys who started the businesses, and reported on why they got all their safety boots from Weber Industrial Supply, but not their wrenches. He thought if he watched their hands that he might appear as a hunter among men who have never hunted. But it was always hard to get the guys to sit down, after they ate the free focus group pizza and had a few Heinekens. Goetzler would have to ask them five or six times.

After he tied his shoes, he looked up to meet eyes with Mike Rosen, the lawyer who almost forced him into group therapy. Rosen sat on a stool and talked into his cell phone while he threw towels on the floor. Melanoma scars flecked his back.

"I paid them extra money to use new paintbrushes," Rosen said into the phone. "The fucking contractor assured me. I have it in writing."

He squinted hard at Goetzler, but Goetzler never rang a bell.

"How do I know?" Rosen said. "Because the brush hairs are dried in my fucking trim. They come off old brushes like that."

Life sure got you, Goetzler thought.

Mike Rosen left the ACLU in 1974 to take dope cases and

cash retainers. The draft was over and his adolescence was never interrupted by Vietnam. He bought the first car phone and parked his red Mercedes in the fire lane outside criminal court. The yellow lines meant nothing like the signs stuck in the sidewalk. He talked loudly with the top down and waved his two-carat pinkie ring at the trustee inmates picking up cigarette butts. He'd tell people about getting oral sex while sailing off Sanibel Island. When the cops asked him to move, he lifted a finger and kept talking. But he had a spastic colon. His fancy Italian shoes were always flat behind a stall door in the second-floor men's room at Cook County Criminal Court. He came out bloated and mean and made juries hate cops like strep throat.

He played juries like a matinee actor who had stock in the show. Goetzler watched him pit the West Side blacks against the South Side Irish in the paneled jury boxes. The tiebreakers were the Puerto Ricans from Chicago Avenue, and they'd bite their tongues to keep from laughing when he got a uniform two seconds away from yelling *Fuck off*. Poppy has something on his mind, they'd say of the cop. A real carbonis. They'd clap for Rosen after the verdict, dancing the samba in their padded chairs. We are the people, they'd sing. Rosen gave them his cards in the hallway and lent quarters for the pop machine.

Goetzler knew Mike Rosen wouldn't remember him, even if reminded. There wasn't a chance. The guy could see Goetzler every day until he went to die in Florida, and nothing would jar loose.

After thirty years, revenge seemed romantic enough that completing the act might make another man finally want Goetzler's moments. But he needed a way to make Rosen see him without Rosen knowing he was looking. Goetzler walked slowly past Mike Rosen and threw his towel in the hamper. They'd been sharing the same gym these years, but coming at different times.

Rosen pointed at Goetzler on the stand and tapped his left tassel loafer, the courtroom hot and airless because Judge Hoey ordered the fans cut for making noise. He looked at the jury while they fanned themselves with notebook paper. He kept his finger aimed at Goetzler's neck. The judge was watching dust motes in the window light. He sweat thick lines from his forehead.

Donald Goetzler didn't have probable cause to arrest Harris Roosevelt, Rosen said, so he shot him.

He smiled and showed white teeth. Some jurors let their eyes close, others nodded. You stay quiet and eat it today, Kerm told Goetzler. Hoey likes to urinate his first Absolut martini by five o'clock at the Drake. He'll push things along. Goetzler stared past Rosen, watching the kid he shot try remembering not to cross his legs. The kid was tall and his crutches leaned against an unused chair. Goetzler couldn't pull him from a pair and thought that forgetting the kid made him more professional. Silence, he thought. He would just sit and look.

We know all about cops like Donald Goetzler, Rosen said.

The lady jurors fanned themselves and nodded. They were heavyset matrons in feathered hats with lace over their sweaty faces and held small purses from Woolworth.

They bring the jungles of Vietnam back to our communities, he said. He just shot this kid in an alley.

Goetzler heard a few jurors a-huh. The kid's neck sagged from sleep.

Our children are not the Viet Cong, Rosen said.

The jurors mouthed no. Some even half said it.

Your Honor, Rosen said, I move you dismiss this case on the grounds of police misconduct. I also request that the court require Officer Donald Goetzler to undergo psychological testing before returning to duty. Judge Hoey banged his gavel. Request granted, he said. He wiped his face with the sleeve of his black robe. It was four o'clock in the afternoon and his hands were shaking. Goetzler rose from the stand while three Mexicans snuck into the courtroom with burritos. No matter what happens, Kerm told him, we got the fix.

8

It rained when the airport taxi turned down avenue Foch, a cold slanting rain, the way it rained when Annie stood on the gum stains at Charles de Gaulle Airport, forgetting the cop, and how he didn't run last night with the streetlight in his sweatshirt. In the cab, Raymond Poincaré became Malakoff, and the city disappeared between wiper passes. There was only the Arab, herself, and his eyes rising into the rearview mirror. She drew the coat over her legs, and didn't think about the cop running, or the way his eyes stuck to the ground. Paris was time for the quiet. Dreaming, she thought, kept you from living.

Without notice, Annie left Nick for short weeks like this, five days every four months, but never in the summer. Then, it was her heels on the Gold Coast sidewalks, Erie, Ontario, Chestnut with the cars' headlights against bumpers, the virgin daiquiris with hedge fund managers from Atlanta, road time with Bobby up to the North Shore where oncologists paid big money to love her like a dream wife. Paris was long walks with headphones and Billie Holiday, *love that's fresh and still unspoiled*, and the Peugeots with hard clutches going fast past the Invalides. Billie Holiday's eyes lifted her until she thought herself the golden leaves. For five days, it was only she and the music: Gerry Mulligan and Stan Getz, their sounds like waves hitting rocks, the feral, bent notes of John Coltrane, Bill Evans making the silence loud enough to lilt. She wore the headset and didn't talk for the week. Not a word. She played mute for the hotel staff and carried a notepad and wrote what she wanted in her University of Illinois French.

In Paris, she liked being jazz. Just one loud silence.

Goetzler and hotel johns gave her Dizzy Gillespie and "Night in Tunisia" on an iPod, and hot peppermint tea while the altitude winds pushed night clouds from O'Hare to de Gaulle. There were walks along Raymond Poincaré with the shop windows wet from the October storms, perfumed lotion in glass jars, a king-size room at Le Parc Mur, smuggled joints smoked slowly in hot baths, Miles Davis playing in the taxicab, his horn tense like cats about to fight, and the driver speeding across Pont d'Iena in the early night. They got her these five days.

The wind quit her last afternoon and the fading light turned oddly warm. The people walked up the Trocadero steps in their coats from the morning. She crossed to the left and walked along the brown Seine. Some pouty Germans went by in a tourist boat, then the winds came again. The river turned choppy and the current went sideways into the stern but the old men remained on the top deck, their hands upon the railings. She held her sunglasses to her face and wondered which men would try offering extra money to dig feces from her rectum. There was no way of guessing the type who'd ask. The first guy who did, a Lincoln Park intellectual property lawyer, inquired while he picked a toddler's juice cup off the dining-room table. Is a hundred dollars enough, he said. There was a picture of his green-eyed wife, a wedding shot, some gazebo in the suburbs with Honda Accords passing in the background. It was on the mantel, the wall up the stairway, the nightstand. Annie had seen the picture for three paid hours and forgot the woman's face every time she looked away.

Later, Annie sat on the Metro, the number ten to Place d'Italie, watching the people bounce in the next car. Only the windows truly moved, twisting and raising, but the people bounced the same.

In Vietnamese, Annie's name was Vu Le Thuy, tornado teardrop, the family name written first. Her father believed the hard wind came before all. Huong meant perfume and a river the emperors once watched. Annie was wet on cheeks.

The woman from the Lutheran church, her foster mother, held up a card with her name written on it. Le Thuy in thick black letters. It was the cue for Annie to pronounce her name slowly. She practiced for the women that came for coffee, gray ladies with hard hair and plastic flower arrangements on their kitchen tables. She made Annie understand about going slow by moving her fingers like they walked. Le Thuy, Annie mumbled. She breathed twice between the two words of her name.

It is poetry, the ladies said. Pure poetry.

The woman never called her Annie, but she kept a special Annie room with posters from the musical. There were small dolls still in boxes. Three stuffed dogs. She'd sit in the room, her blue housecoat losing velour, and play an eight-track of the original score. She only sang certain lines, then hummed and stared at Andrea McArdle's autographed headshot, smiling as if the actress's mother. Her husband yelled for her to close the door. She heard nothing but the music and hugged a stuffed dog.

"I love you, tomorrow," she sang.

He put cotton in his ears and turned up the TV. He liked shows about wild animals—the power of a mongoose's jaw, the way badgers mate—and he sat up in his La-Z-Boy when lions got a zebra, wolves an elk. He'd smile and point at the screen with his cigarette. There it is, he'd say. All you need to know about anything.

The man was a master sergeant when he retired from the air force. Just a master sergeant, he told people, not a chief. In 1966, he helped build the airstrip at Phu Bai and hauled dirt in a dump truck through Hue City ten years before Annie was born. That was why she lived in Watega, Illinois, eating homemade beef stew with the man and his wife, and watching the sunlight streak the field mud outside the kitchen window. He bet he drove dirt right past this girl's house. He got to know Hue City like a frequented diner. The woman's face was round, her hair stiff, and she nodded while her husband spoke. She played the organ at Good Shepherd Lutheran where the pastor was hoping to sponsor a boat person. He asked for volunteers on a cold Easter Sunday in March.

"Christians know Christians by their circumcised hearts," he said. "It is our mark."

That's what Debbie needs, the man thought of his wife. She sat in the room, singing all night with an afghan across her legs. It was time to find her something else.

After breakfast, the man left for diner coffee and the woman brought down the eight-track deck. She played the songs in the kitchen while she wiped off the unused toaster. "It's the Hard-Knock Life" was Annie's signal to come downstairs in costume, a red dress, white tights, and black patent leather shoes. She'd slept in curlers, rolled tightly because the curl hadn't been taking. She then danced so her shoes tapped the white floor. The woman smiled and folded her hands together.

"You've never seen the show," she said, "but you know the dance exactly. Bless your heart."

Annie went until the woman finished wiping the counter and turned off the tape. Her legs felt like fell sticks. She watched the woman bend over and clean the scuff marks with a green pad. Her housecoat went to her knees.

"It just baffles me how you can know," the woman said.

When the phone started after *The Price Is Right,* the woman sat on the couch, taking the calls like short orders. The cushions were covered in plastic and held the window light. They are boat people, she'd tell them, making the syllables with her fingers. Boat people.

Annie sat on the steps, watching herself in her shoe toes. The woman's cat had six kittens and they were colored the same white as her kitchen floor. They slept in a large box by the back door. If you touch those babies, the woman translated from a book, you'll kill one. She'd scribbled the Vietnamese words on lined paper. Annie looked up from her shoes where the mother cat lay outside the box, licking her teats. She wanted to put her face in the box, letting the kittens climb up her neck, then slide back down. She would smile with her face in the blanket. But she sat upon her hands, listening to the woman's fast voice, and imagined the kittens' unopened eyes while they walked over themselves. They will die, the woman had written out. Tuan Li. She underlined the phrase.

Goetzler cooked Annie dinner but she never ate with him. She waited in her heels while he sliced shallots, using his knife precisely.

He basted pork loin with balsamic vinegar, and zested lemon into a saucepan. She looked at the screen of her cell phone while he flamed scallops in a sauté pan. He'd been making fun of men who won medals and wore them. She found he loved doing it more than anything.

"I have a Silver Star," he said. "But I never once wore the commemorative tie tack."

All of them had won something, Annie thought.

"I worked with people who would have laughed in my face if I wore it," he said. "They don't understand what happened back then like we do. South Vietnam was a democracy and they wouldn't let us save it."

"I was born after the war," she said.

"But you knew South Vietnamese army veterans?"

"I knew men who would kill, but not fight. That is why the North won."

"Did your father fight for the South?"

"My father kept stacks of old *Playboy* magazines left by the Americans. He kept them wrapped in rice paper to protect them from the humidity. The Viet Cong were reading Ho Chi Minh's poems and the Saigon soldiers looked at *Playboy*. I think my father was a man who would kill, but never fight."

Goetzler looked at her in the window glass, and sipped pinot noir from Oregon. The windows wrapped around the room, the lake and the sky half the walls. She moved so that she was by herself in a panel while he thought to speak. If she stared long enough, he'd be quiet until she talked.

After dinner, they sat on the leather couch and Goetzler's bourbon and Rolex caught the lamplight. He looked at his bookshelf, French poets and histories of the Civil War. He then turned on the CD player with a remote. It was piano jazz, the usual theme music for divorced retired men, but without the scotch-on-the-rocks melancholy. Annie thought Monk, then not, knowing that Monk made her darkness go light, but he never walked her across a still lake. This was Bill Evans, the song "Gloria's Step," and she loved how the bass man made her the raindrops.

"Remembering music," he said. "Bill Evans has a way of keeping you in your head without getting you lonely. On our first date, you told me that."

I never thought I'd see you again, Annie thought. She said, "You have a nice place."

"I'm pretty poetic for a professional soldier, wouldn't you think?"

"I don't think you like jazz," she said.

Annie watched him rattle his ice cubes off the glass like he didn't hear her. Goetzler was getting ready to narrate his life like a retired mercenary, always a man who knew men, and his illusions about seeing them had been stripped away long ago. Cynicism has a few pillows, he'd say. Cuban cigars. Hine Cognac. Call girls.

He talked of grabbing Stasi agents in West Berlin, then giving them fruit and coffee, and refusing toilet breaks unless they talked. Men broke after shitting themselves in front of women agents, he said. Goetzler, according to himself, once ran the night in 1970s Berlin, using ex-Gestapo to light the Reds on fire. Last time, he told Annie that the ultimate revenge was living well: this was it, flesh for gold, but you beat them by eating in better restaurants. Some men saved six months to have an hour with her, but Goetzler paid every week, telling her how this act was biology for him, and that cost. But, he'd say, there's poetry in the way cells move.

She knew Goetzler read more than he ever saw, and that women didn't like him. It was the pout behind his smile.

He picked up a pipe from the glass end table. The stem was dented from his teeth. Annie bet he smoked nights and watched himself in the windows.

"I bought this in Hong Kong on Carmel Road," he said. "The British officers went there for blended tobacco. My platoon sergeant, this old guy named Olszewski, gave me the money for it. He bet me General Loan wouldn't shoot that Viet Cong. We were sitting in our jeep, eating *pho ga* from our steel pots, then he shot him like he was turning off his office light. I saw the most famous picture of the war being taken."

Annie watched Goetzler tap tobacco down into the bowl. All her dates had seen something: Michael Jordan spottings on Rush Street, Oprah running the treadmill at the East Bank Club.

"You know the picture?" Goetzler said.

She nodded.

"Doesn't the war mean anything to you?"

Annie looked in his eyes without seeing him.

"I forgot my Vietnamese for a reason," she said.

Goetzler bit the pipe and showed her the picture in a book. General Nguyen Ngoc Loan held the chrome-plated .38 after shooting the Viet Cong. The man's face was contorting, his head tilted from the force of the round. The plaid shirt. The black shorts. Saigon in white light and dust.

"General Loan was no brute. He was an air force officer and acted French with his cigarettes. We'd have dinner with his staff at the Rex Hotel."

She looked away so he'd wait for her to speak. She never heard him set down the book. The older men used whatever they'd just read to instruct her: hardcover histories, the sports page, George Will syndicated in the *Sun-Times*.

In college, a political science professor named Balbus put Eddie Adams's picture on the overhead. He used a pencil, showing where you could see the bullet passing out of the Viet Cong's temple. With this picture, he said, we brought the Military Industrial Complex down. Balbus permed his gray hair, wore turquoise rings, and thought the problem was the patriarchy. Annie let him touch her for grades, but only through her panties, and ran up his American Express for room service sea bass and crème brûlée. He'd stroke her hip with his finger, his eyes like tops. You are a poetic people, he'd say.

Goetzler lit the tobacco. He drew the pipe hard and his face went orange.

"That VC General Loan shot was like Osama Bin Laden," he said. "The VC had killed the wives and children of his staff officers right that morning. The guy who took the picture was sorry he ruined General Loan's life with it."

Annie looked at her phone. It was programmed to play hearts, free cell, mine sweeper.

"General Loan tried to run a pizza place in Virginia," he said. "They shut him down. These are the same people who sold out your country. They all got law degrees. That should scare people."

She smiled and got up and walked to the bathroom. He looked at her like a watch.

"Excuse me," she said.

What did this matter. She was from Watega, Illinois, where the luckiest men got to drink at the Elks Lodge. For her, Vietnam was four memories. Goetzler tapped the weight into his pipe bowl.

His toilet was white and public-looking but pine-oil clean. He had a yellow pad full of geometry problems by the stool, towels the same color as the sink, a CD player with classical music, Chopin and Brahms. She sat on the floor and played a full game of hearts against her cell phone. She took ten minutes and knew he wouldn't say a word.

9

Mike Spence drove the paddy wagon along Racine and rolled up his window ahead of the rain. Denny Collins still looked at the cell phone, wanting his medical profile extended, his face fat making his red eyes slits. He gave it a test ring by thumbing a button. The rain came sideways through the window and spotted the *Sun-Times* on his lap before he rolled it up without watching himself. He looked hit by a wrinkle bomb, one fat slouch with a Starbucks fetish. He dropped a daily twenty on key lime squares, wild berry scones, crumble berry cake, then spent twenty more for double mocha lattes. He checked his voice mail and nothing came up.

"It's the job that gave me the heart attacks," he said. "The doctor told the department. What good am I out here?"

Mike turned down Altgeld where the cars were parked tightly along the curbs. The parking tickets they wrote that morning were soaked beneath the wiper blades. Mike went slow and checked for zone stickers.

Collins opened the *Sun-Times* and studied the television listings like the Dow results. Mike turned up Racine and then left on

Belmont, passing the punk rock holdouts drinking coffee at Dunkin' Donuts, their tattooed necks against the wet windows.

"This heart medicine makes me piss all the time," Collins said.

Mike watched the rain slant into the gangways between the rehabbed graystones. Collins was eligible for disability at forty, eighty percent of seventy grand a year for life. He wanted it like some men wanted detective. He called people he knew. He walked the paperwork between desks downtown. You want to mess with Collins? Nowacki once said to Mike. You tell him he's being promoted.

"Now they got me on the wagon," he said. "I didn't hit a lawyer like you did. How can I carry bodies down stairs?"

Mike watched the clouds press the rooftops.

"The doctor says I could be having little heart attacks right now. I wouldn't even know."

"He said that?"

"They come that fast."

"You stay in the car," Mike said.

"I could get you killed in a real situation. How could I back you up?"

He dipped a cinnamon scone into his mocha latte and took a bite. The crumbs stuck to his mouth corners.

"These things don't get soft enough," he said.

"Leave it in there longer," Mike said.

"Then it breaks apart. You got blueberries floating around in your coffee like little eyeballs."

Collins talked to his reflection in the window. His jowls were pocked and cleated. The scone dripped and the wet crumbs plopped on the newspaper and blotched the ink.

"I tried a muffin," he said. "You dunk them once and it's a mess."

Mike drove and watched the power lines snap in the wind. The wagon was his assignment for smacking Todd in the alley. Kenjuan Mills got him three years of carrying bodies out of three-flats and flex-cuffing drunks after street festivals. There would be different guys where Collins sat, some so fat they lived to un-Velcro their body armor, and a few with acid reflux disease and a bad habit of not covering their mouths, but Mike would be driving the wagon for a long time.

10

The night before Uncle Kerm left the nursing home, the nurses shined his alligator suitcases with paste wax and packed his clothes. Goetzler looked at the old TWA stickers from Tahiti and Rio de Janeiro while his uncle lay watching Jennifer Moore and *The Wall Street Minute* on Fox Newschannel. Outside the lake was furious and the waves came over the seawalls at Belmont and Lake Shore Drive.

"She's got great fister tits," Kerm said of the commentator. "You know that?"

Goetzler vaguely looked at the television. He let himself be slow in answering Kerm. The lagged response, he knew, branded him either homosexual or autistic in Kerm's eyes. But Goetzler loved Kerm because he was facing the end better than his brother had. Al Goetzler died in a hospital, crying beside an expressionless wife.

"Jesus, Donny," his uncle said. "And you wonder why some guys think you are gay."

Goetzler laughed.

"She's got great tits," Kerm said.

"Just like fists."

"Sure."

In the morning, a chartered medical jet was flying Kerm to Naples, Florida, from Meigs Field. He'd rented space in a nursing home by the ocean on the money from selling eight Lincoln Park three-flats in 1995. The police department gave him a desk and a phone so he bought real estate all through the seventies.

"You'll come back in the summer," Goetzler said.

"Right to this room."

"What if there's a dying guy in it."

"My lawyer says they'll have to move him."

Uncle Kerm wasn't serious, but he used his money to entertain himself. Alaska cruises for heart patients, beachside nursing homes, and getting his way in restaurants. The yuppies buying his three-flats had made him a very wealthy man.

"I saw Mike Rosen today," Goetzler said. "We've been at the same gym for thirty years, but were coming at different times."

Kerm had *Investor's Business Daily* spread across his lap. He was underlining the symbols for his stocks with a ballpoint. Jennifer Moore had finished *The Wall Street Minute*.

"Do like Chuck Murphy, Donny," he said. "Sell that fancy condo and go soak it up somewhere. A hooker will take care of Rosen. Cocaine made the guy a two-stroke."

"Rosen doesn't recognize me," Goetzler said. "This is a good opportunity to make him understand what he opened."

Without looking from his paper, Kerm waved Goetzler away with his hand.

"What he opened? Now Murphy's a guy who should have a fight with Rosen. All those years Chuck defended the same mopes, but Rosen just got the ones who could pay cash. You were offered a generous deal and you turned it down to make money. Chucky fought hard to help the shitbirds. And he really liked helping them. It was an honor to have that marine sweat you in court."

Goetzler ate it and smiled at Kerm, amazed the man could underline stock symbols without glasses. In fact, his vision remained 20-20, and if his heart was strong, Goetzler believed he could barrel roll his old Mustang fighter plane. Though, he couldn't do it with the Camel between his teeth anymore. But ten years ago, Uncle Kerm could still dogfight with some Luftwaffe veteran who'd become a West Berlin cop after the war. They'd duel one last time over the Tuscan olive groves and Renaissance villas, where Machiavelli learned to survive, and Goetzler would like to watch through binoculars when the German forced Kerm to parachute.

Goetzler shadowed Mike Rosen through Lincoln Park with the picture of Nguyen Ngoc Loan shooting the Viet Cong in his pocket. He tailed him down Armitage where he headed for the restaurant bars, the Caribbean bistros, and Mongolian barbecues. Rosen couldn't stand straight, but he never lost his grin. Goetzler figured he'd study the old lawyer and think of how to work the picture into any revenge dream.

He followed him into a retroactive piano lounge where the player was on break. Rosen sat down at the bar and started chatting the blondes, their hair wound in comb clamps. Goetzler knew they were ten grand high on Visa cards for shoes, sushi, and useless weekends at the Soho Grand in New York. They lived in studio apartments off Surf Street and sold commercial mortgages out in Oak Brook and hoped to hook the guy who would get them pregnant, then hire a nineteen-year-old Croatian girl to push the stroller. Night after night, Goetzler watched Rosen think he was delicious behind his Bombay martini, his silk shirt open two buttons, never hearing the women mouth disco king.

Goetzler saw Rosen every day in the locker room, then later in the bars where quartered women chittered in new shoes. He was a stacked towel to Rosen, an ashtray on a table. He drank his water and lime while Rosen sipped his martini through tight lips. When they met eyes, nothing jarred loose. Goetzler had one of those faces, arid he knew it, his eyes like clean windows that people looked through.

One night, Rosen got scorched.

Five minutes were left for the *Sex and the City* night drink specials when the blonde swung her elbows along the bar. She pushed through the women lined two deep, waving a Visa card. Goetzler watched Rosen lean against the bar and catch eyefuls. She led with her fake D-cups and they steadied their chocolate martinis and sneered. He watched the blonde's chest, his hair made brown again by Just for Men. The women eyed her breasts and then sized their own in the mirror behind the bar. The bartender shook the vodka and poured and knew that the women were past his goatee and tattoos. The air purifier hanging from the ceiling sucked the smoke from their thin cigarettes.

Rosen and the blonde made eye contact before she looked away. She wore diamond earrings but had no ring.

"Put the card away," he said. "I got this."

The blonde wrote a number on a cocktail napkin. She pushed it over without watching herself.

"My landlady usually sits home nights," she said.

The phone number had his prefix. Rosen didn't know what to do with his hands.

"Wait until the doctor you marry leaves you for another broad," he said.

She smiled chilly.

"We'll see what you know then," he said.

The blonde held up her little finger. A cell phone rang in her purse.

She turned away from him and took the call, closing her ear with a fingernail.

Goetzler ordered Glenlivet neat. He lit a Cubano, watching Rosen grin like he had a good segue. Goetzler then walked over and sat next to him. The old lawyer didn't look over. He put the picture of Nguyen Ngoc Loan shooting the Viet Cong beside the ashtray.

"Sir," Goetzler said. "I'll buy you another if you answer a question."

"I drink Bombay Sapphire," Rosen said.

Goetzler drew his cigar and nodded at the ponytailed bartender.

While Rosen was looking at Goetzler, he noticed the print.

"We really shoved it up their asses with that picture," Goetzler lied. "We stopped Nixon cold. We were the fascists and Eddie Adams proved it forever."

Rosen was still looking at the picture. He squinted like this was ordinary, and didn't say a word until the bartender set down his Bombay martini.

"We told ourselves that to feel better," he said. "We stayed in Vietnam four years after the picture rocked the world. I was more afraid of going to Vietnam than I cared about stopping the war."

Goetzler raised his Glenlivet twelve-year-old while Rosen just nodded and drank.

"I'm thinking of licensing this picture and putting it on T-shirts and coffee mugs," Goetzler said. "As a retired marketing executive, I think the punk rock teenagers will co-opt this image and that could mean T-shirts."

"Do you want money?"

"No," Goetzler said. "Just tell me what the picture means to you."

"I could see it as a CD cover," Rosen said. "Some kid band might think they're smart for doing it, too. If they sold, I could see the T-shirts. But the kids wouldn't know what it meant even if it did hit."

"But what does it mean to you?"

"Nothing now. You see worse in the courts."

Looking at Rosen, Goetzler thought, You lucky son of a bitch.

Later, Goetzler followed Rosen home, in the dark, back to his town house where he lived on three floors among Persian rugs, Tiffany lamps, and Vivaldi on surround sound. Goetzler watched from across the street, beneath an umbrella, the rain hitting him under the nylon.

Rosen kicked the puddle if he got his shoes wet, or if he dropped his keys by the stoop steps. Inside, he stripped off his silk shirt in the window, cursing the rain for streaking it. He threw his shoes at the door for getting wet in the puddles. Then, he called for an escort, and if the agency was slow ringing back, he'd throw his cell phone into the sofa pillows.

Goetzler watched Rosen's face contorting. He threw his hand a second time, but the phone was already gone.

Rosen liked ordering sex when the rain leaned past his stained-glass windows. Something about wet girls, Goetzler thought. He left them shivering by the door after they rang the bell, their hair ruined by the weather, the drops leaving dents in their made-up faces. He knew they saw him, shirtless and freckled from Naples,

Florida, pacing his ten-thousand-dollar rugs and talking to no-body on his second cell phone. He wanted the girls to see him for a full two minutes while the lake wind drove the rain sideways. Even though Rosen loved to call hookers, he believed he was bet-ter than them. And there'd be an issue about the price. Goetzler was sure the agency warned him about this. The prices were fixed, all-inclusive, and he could reach his goal multiple times. That was all they ever said on the phone. But there were always new women, skinny blondes in business suits, black girls in platform shoes. He made them dance braless in the window like he wanted people to see.

The next night, Goetzler waited in the Jeep Cherokee after Rosen walked the block to the restaurant bars. He did not hear the rain. He was listening to the *Nick Adams Stories* on tape. Hemingway had taught him how to stop the room from spinning when he was drunk, the proper way for holding a newspaper at a café table, even how a man should look at hills and trees. But Hemingway didn't work in Vietnam, even though Goetzler tried. The martinis tasted funny in Southeast Asia because the Vietnam-ese bartenders never got the vermouth right. After the story "The Battler," Goetzler stepped from the Jeep and crossed the street with his hands in the pockets of his leather coat, thinking himself Nick Adams when he first noticed his hurt knee from the brake-man slugging him off the train.

There were red stickers on Rosen's windows from Windy City Security Systems on Kedzie. Goetzler went around the back and pitched alley stones at the glass, then waited. No flashing lights or alarm sirens. He pushed against the back door, and waited again. There was nothing.

He returned two nights later, after learning Rosen's routine. He came with a glass-cutter and took out the window in the back door, then reached through and let himself inside. It was the kitchen, a big white room with an eight-burner stove, a rotisserie spit built into its own enclave, and black marble countertops. He worked a Maglite against the floor, looking for dog food bowls.

He carried in the backpack only what he needed: one rolled picture of Nguyen Ngoc Loan shooting the Viet Cong, Scotch tape, a pair of black shorts, a plaid madras shirt, and military police handcuffs. He forgot sandals, but he wasn't sure the Viet Cong even wore them. The .38 was between his belt and his coat, a pearl-handled revolver like Loan's. Back in 1968, he'd been in Saigon the day the Tet Offensive hit and Eddie Adams got the famous picture. Goetzler was one street over, on Tu Ten Loc, looking for his glasses on the floor of the Jeep. His nose had been sweaty and Sergeant Olszewski braked too fast. He didn't know about the picture until the next day, but he told guys how he watched the general raise the pistol, and that he even bummed a cigarette from a one-eyed staff officer after the VC fell backward.

In the Maglite beam, he saw Tiffany lamps, ten to a room, vases from Ming dynasties, a Matisse pastel above the fireplace. The windows were framed in stained glass, and the white rugs lay over hardwood floors. Rosen had cabinets of Hummels, the little German girls in dresses, the small boys with watering cans.

Goetzler followed the beam back to Rosen's office. Last week, the lawyer bought a desk that Grover Cleveland used in his law practice after his presidency. He told the locker room. Goetzler figured Rosen hid his cash retainers like this. The money was all in things.

He emptied the backpack over the desk and put it back on. He lay the picture beside the desk lamp, leaving the shorts and the shirt upon stacked paper, then turned on the small light before reclining in Rosen's swivel chair. He put his feet up, waiting a minute before removing the pistol from his holster. He lit the desk lamp.

Uncle Kerm would laugh about this stunt. Goetzler saw himself getting points with the old man.

You made him dress up like the VC in that picture, he'd say. You even wore a William Westmoreland mask? I bet Rosen's colon hasn't stopped since you left him shaking. I'll bet he won't speak a word about it. The cops aren't his friends.

Kerm would beat the table with his fist, and howl like he did telling Goetzler how his father got kicked out of the navy for messing himself. He messed them standing in the chow line at Great Lakes, he said, and he messed them nightly in his rack while he dreamed of his guitar and his Bill Monroe seventy-eights and the few times the rodeo came to Lake County. You should have seen him around our mother. Your old man held the yarn while she balled it.

11

The work made Annie nervy when she couldn't stop imagining the date that might kill her: a cell phone salesman from Libertyville in the city on his day off, or an old man with five divorces. Her last sight may be Days Inn wallpaper, or the granite countertops in a Wicker Park loft. She started believing all her dates would strangle her. But playing Goetzler eased her fear, and made her so arrogant she believed herself beyond the edge of things.

Some nights, she even alleged she wasn't afraid to die, and that made her free beyond the world's understanding.

But tonight, she had a new client, a young, unmarried futures trader on Randolph Street, and she got scared thinking that a man without a reason to see a hooker might be the snuff john. All afternoon, she walked her apartment and imagined him piling hundred-dollar bills on the table while she explained how she won't be bound. She'd threaten to leave, but he'd keep dropping them like the cards of a winning poker hand, his face Viagra red.

The anxiety was making her hands shake. The cats ran away when she tried petting them. Since lunch, she jumped at distant sirens, crow caws, and the windy raindrops against her window.

She even called Nick three times, the fat guy whose real name was Larry. If she canceled, he'd pitch Goetzler the other Vietnamese girl who called herself Charlize. Annie then tried sweeping the floor, but kept dropping the broom, and decided it was time to stop being a cat. She phoned Nick telling him she'd take her chances with Goetzler.

"That's your call," he said, "but these older guys don't mind the variety."

Annie didn't care. She knew things about Goetzler that Nick would spend seven lifetimes trying to figure out. Goetzler wanted to believe he fought for something in Vietnam, and Annie was the gatekeeper to that wish. He needed her thank you, or the men who burned their draft cards would always be right. Vietnam might finally pay. Annie then turned off her cell phone and took a nap with her cats and dreamed that the world was an ice rink.

She woke and took the yoga book from the shelf. It slipped away. She followed the book with her hands until it lay open on the floor. Immediately, the blond, white woman was holding the dying warrior position, her chin upon her shin. Annie envied her calm and cried because yoga failed to ever quiet her mind. Her fingers always felt like the running legs of different people. But she calmed her hands by reminding herself that she wasn't a cat anymore, scared of stray noise, and then decided this North Dakotan in Manhattan had never entertained a thought louder than a popping champagne cork.

She tried sleeping, but couldn't keep her hands still for longer than an hour. They ground the feathers in her pillow before knocking her water glass off the nightstand. When she couldn't hold a blanket corner, she got up, went to the front room, and tried staying her fingers by splaying them on the window glass.

Posing for the cop, like the summer nights, might calm her

hands, but his window was rainy dark, and he was off on a long run. His woman was gone because the candles never lit the windows, and men never thought of those details unless a hooker was coming over. But watching the cop run was better than posing, and made her forget she had hands. She imagined him a dog, a German shepherd, who could be ordered into emotions.

Sometimes, the cop went south first, and ran calmly, but if he started north into the city, he came back like a boxer, throwing restrained punches at the darkness: the one-two, but never a third jab. She didn't want love from him. She knew closeness with an open heart would make him too real, and he'd cease calming her hands on the nights she must work. He must stay beyond the window.

12

Mike ran down Cornelia, beneath the Ravenswood Metro tracks, and watched blond men wind Christmas lights around their town house fences. They laced the cords with garlands. The night was also good for running, humid cool between the rains. The men weren't smiling, and they strung the lights like soldiers did concertina wire while wives watched from windows, so he turned back toward the lake, relieved he could add three more miles without having to explain the extra time later. He started to look back, but stopped himself, knowing the men would remind him how he didn't miss the riddle-life he and Susan led after the abortion.

But Mike never let himself think this very long. His pace would slow and he'd not sleep later because his body felt cheated and awake. He'd start missing her toes against his ankle, and soon he'd remember that he lay beside her many nights wishing her a random lover. In the beginning, he'd tell himself, he was sure neither one of them did that. Now, there were places he was learning not to go.

The wind quit off the lake and he was sweating in a long-sleeved T-shirt. He ran in the street, but stayed close to the parked

cars. There were more men stringing Christmas lights and garlands, disgusted men, and they all worked like their neighbors. He
cut down the first alley, hoping to keep his mind on the streetlit
puddles, not the decorators, but it was too late. He'd already
started remembering the last year of his marriage.

The medical examiner told Mike that Susan hadn't felt a
thing. The killer swung the baseball bat and she just died. It was
painless for her, he said.

She was gone six months now. No cops asked Mike if he
missed her. They looked at him in the precinct's locker room like
they would a guy at the YMCA. There was little to gain by knowing the wagon driver.

He kept quiet and spent his days driving domestic batterers
and car thieves to bond court, letting the silence of her death drone
with the arrestee's heel knocks against the wagon walls. He'd sometimes forget by looking at blond women in Volvo wagons, and
imagining himself feeling as convinced about things as them, but
Susan always returned behind his eyes.

Mike hated knowing she died when they were straining to see
love in each other, and his mother-in-law reminded him with a
Christmas card. Thinking of Suzy, she wrote. He smelled her Ben-
son and Hedges on the envelope and remembered how mother
and daughter sat at the kitchen table and imagined the ways
they'd die. Susan went in a motorcycle accident on a warm country night, but her mother saw herself all alone in a room. He also
hated knowing his wife blinked her eyes in a rainy alley and never
opened them. Her last sight may have been a car lot fence, he
thought.

At University of Illinois, where Mike studied on the GI Bill,
he first saw Susan walking through yellow leaves, Ophelia in a
black skirt, her eyes brown like Illinois rivers. She sat on bar stools

beside him and listened to his Fort Bragg stories, drinking Glen-livet, while he told her about how in 1988 a C-130 full of para-troopers exploded on a demonstration jump for their families, and how he and Dilger manned a drop zone water point and watched the bodies fall on fire with the wives and the little sisters. Later, Dilger and he never talked about it; they just got drunk off-post and found hookers in a tobacco field house trailer; and neither Dilger nor he could look at each other right forever after. They'd seen themselves on fire.

Mike wanted to make the rich pay. Somehow, their young never fall and burn.

Susan understood. Back in her Illinois town, her father, a short sheet-metal worker with a squirrel head, beat her when he was laid off longer than a week. He fought in Korea with the USMC, freez-ing in the Chosin Reservoir with Chesty Puller, and never got over having survived a forgotten war. He claimed nobody knew how to listen. Susan got drunk and gave the reasons for her beatings, but never the details. The morning she wouldn't eat pancakes, the time she wore makeup at twelve. Her mother could remember none of it. But Mike loved her because they both had eyes that were as cu-rious as they were afraid of life, and she never turned away his sto-ries. She felt his slurred words, but ran home conflicted after last call. On the bar, she'd leave her poems about clotheslines, airport roads, and dry cleaners that press the stains in farther. She wasn't comfortable explaining herself.

They came together. They ran from each other. They crossed paths like this for ten years, the stakes getting higher. One day, af-ter the book sold, they got married at City Hall between Cuban and Sri Lankan couples, and spent two nights at the Hilton and Towers having the best sex of their lives. Susan missed her period the next month.

But Mike Spence believed himself a tough guy until his thirty-fifth birthday. He'd walked into the blurry waste of the Mojave Desert, pack mule fashion, one dreamy grunt among many. Before meeting Susan, he soldiered in Honduras and Panama; he ran triathlons, competed in power lifting, boxed at The Windy City Gym, covered dope at federal court, and backpacked through the Balkans after the war. But it did nothing against the sadness of seeing Susan thirteen years after the yellow leaves, the abortion having broken her in her weak places because he wrote a novel about soldiers who got sad after watching their buddies burn in the sky. *We saw ourselves on fire, he'd tell her. My father beat me when Chicago lost to Green Bay, she told him, and I was getting potato chip crumbs on the couch.*

Whenever he forgot Susan and let himself remember running the Sacré Coeur steps with Dilger, he wished he could time the lapses. It would help him gauge his progress in forgetting her. But Parisian leave with Dilger and the French girls who feigned repulsion to their dog tags was something he couldn't let himself remember either. He guessed Dilger wasn't Dilger anymore, the handsome son of the dirty-crude oil fields, but something kept him from calling his mother in Burkburnett, Texas, and checking to see if he'd recovered from the night the MP sticked him. If Dilger had, Mike would only feel weaker.

Mike ran across Irving Park and passed Orange Garden Chop Suey, the last of the neon-lit takeaways. He drew the cold air without coughing, and became all body, his stride longer, more deliberate.

He turned down the alley and the pole lamps were bright in the puddles. When he found himself sliding on his knees, he couldn't remember going down. The asphalt barked his shins and he stopped himself with his hands. He breathed and spat before turning to see legs stuck before a rat-proof garbage can.

The woman was small and Asian. She lay on her back with closed eyes, her tiny shoulders lost in a trench coat. He crawled over and pushed her hair from her eyes, the thin wet strands, but they never opened. He touched her dripping throat. He put his ear to her chest, pulling away when it rose and touched him.

Looking at her, he thought of cut flowers. He stood while the puddle water diluted his knee blood.

"Hey," he said.

The rain hit her forehead where she lay quiet, her head on blue-bagged newspapers.

He bent down again and touched her shoulder, then shook it, but her head rolled left. He looked at her neck, head, the stomach of her trench coat. There was no blood. He put his nose to her mouth, smelling for liquor, but she was clean. When he stood with her, he thought he held a cat. He'd decided to sprint for Ravenswood Hospital when she said, "You'd remember me without my trench coat."

Her eyes opened and they held the alley light. She looked at him without blinking.

Mike knew it was the woman from across the street. She left the windows when Susan died and he forgot imagining the tautness of her body. She was strong, small, and smelled like scented candles.

"You keep your head," she said. "I like that. You are a good soldier."

"How do you know I was a soldier?" he said.

"It is the way you run," she said. "Your upper body never moves. I always wonder if you run with a quarter between your teeth."

He didn't know how to answer the woman, but it felt good holding her. He was walking now and the rain had started small and warm. He hoped she wouldn't ask to be let down.

"Soldiers are quiet," she said. "Cops are loud. That is another way I know."

"That's not always true."

"Sure," she said. "Soldiers are younger and lack confidence. You all stay confused and that keeps you from speaking quickly."

"I don't know about that."

"You are confused enough to keep carrying me," she said.

"You haven't told me you are not hurt," he said. "I will carry you until then."

"I think you've wanted to carry me for a long time."

Mike stopped and let the rain disappear into them.

"Let me down," she said.

He watched the woman walk between two garages, lay on the wet leaves fallen from the black trees, then open her trench coat. Her knees raised and her feet turned flat. She wore a white T-shirt and it was quickly wet.

"You know me now," she said.

Mike did, but he kept quiet. The night was warm for the time of year.

He guessed the woman a hooker. She looked at him with eyes that gave orders. He'd dreamed them softer, maybe a girl looking for a way back to the village, but not such a porno dream. After he lay with her, she rubbed her lips with her finger and nodded in the direction of what she wanted pleasured, then smiled and licked her teeth when he complied.

They lay on the leaves a long time. For a while, he didn't even hear the barking dogs. He kept looking for the village in her eyes, but they only mirrored his own.

———

Mike idled the paddy wagon outside the precinct house on Addison. The morning light had come windy, but not cold. He was watching the street dry and waiting for his partner-of-the-day.

Last night, he hadn't gotten the woman's name, but he touched her and kissed her hips. The rain washed her from him between the times they made love, and she kept moving like she knew it. You sprint now, she said. Your legs stretch and I want you to carry me.

The woman made him swim and he'd never felt he expended any effort to please her. Lying with her, he forgot Susan. She gave him a lapse from all of it, but he decided to take her only when she came. He couldn't get used to the quiet mind she gave him. There were still many things to remember.

This morning, he was hoping for a partner-of-the-day he could like, the way he did every morning, just a guy who might use running shoes and read something about the Civil War, enough Shelby Foote to debate whether Stonewall Jackson was fragged at Chancellorsville, or shot by nervous sentries. They'd drive and weigh the variables. Jackson had marched his men barefoot through the Shenandoah, in icy mud and spring snow, making thirty miles a day and surprising federal cavalry so often that General Hooker couldn't believe the Stonewall brigade didn't ride horses. The men might have hated Jackson enough to shoot him off his horse where he sucked lemons against his constant nausea. He did execute deserters, and refused his men whiskey, but he tried teaching them to read. Mike would argue either side. The debate could make the day a minute.

Sometimes, Mike wished he drove the streets with Dilger and they both felt the way they did at nineteen. Dog soldiers, amateur drunks, and free to blow off home and spend leave in Paris. In Mike's dream, he never watched Dilger get sticked by the MPs, but they were older and somehow better read. He thought them warrior poets in the classical sense, like Dennis Hopper said in the movie. They'd seen the boys fall ablaze, but Dilger was never made goofy by a beating.

The women were walking for the El at Sheffield, the working rush that died after 8:20, a hundred young ones in Donna Karan from T.J.Maxx, all heading toward bank jobs on LaSalle Street and the bottle-eyed Board of Trade guys who drank beer with lunch. They held their skirts down against the wind while the cops got out of the double-parked squads with handled thermoses, changing shifts, the midnight guys having warmed the seats through the long morning dark. Blow wind, Mike knew they were thinking. Let those skirts fly up to their necks.

He was trying to imagine white see-throughs when Petersen got into the wagon. He was the partner-of-the-day, a pretend lifer who sold stereos until he was thirty-one, then became a cop when he lost sixty-five grand day trading in the week after 9/11. He wore blue uniform pants, the creases like cleavers, and Mike could see the wet marks on his fly from urine afterdrip.

"The navy taught me how not to piss on my hands," Petersen said.

He took off his hat. Mike waited to pull into traffic. Women drove by in Caravans and Navigators with baby-on-board stickers in the back windows.

"You know why?" Petersen said.

"No," Mike said. "Why couldn't you piss on your hands?"

"So I wouldn't have to waste time washing them."

He smiled at Mike like he'd told the punch line that made the spots seem routine.

"The navy's pretty ingenious," he said.

"They taught you something good."

"If you don't wash your hands," he said, "you can save a full minute on any head call. It was losing the navy money."

This guy was a slider, Mike thought, a little hamburger that comes boxed and speckled with rehydrated onions. He'd tell you how he got blabby drunk at summer day games, drilling Wrigley Field Budweiser in paper cups, while the Irish tricolor tattooed on his ankle got red from a sunburn. He trolled the bleachers, the people talking on cell phones between Sosa at-bats, and looked for two girls sitting alone, blondes with brunettes. Petersen always played to the dark hair: maybe she'd been bulimic because she was more Joyce Dewitt than Suzanne Somers and the crumbs weren't crumbs to her. I'm a cop, he'd say. The women always paid attention until they understood there was no trouble.

Mike drove the wagon down Addison while Petersen used a napkin from Starbucks to dry the wet spots near his fly. It left flecks of white on the blue wool, but he kept rubbing harder.

"You know," Petersen said, "this wagon detail isn't being a cop."

"That's true."

"You just cart bodies and wet drunks."

"Seven hours' worth."

"You don't get to help people on the wagon."

"You're right."

"I bet no woman asks you for directions in this thing."

"One time, but she was in a hurry."

"Mills isn't loved. You could get off this."

"I know what I have to do here," Mike said.

He wanted to tell Petersen that the job had a rhythm, a mind-away-from-the-body buzz, but he'd wait to use this explanation on a cop he might like. The guy would laugh, maybe tease him about being a new age goof. You're just left of magical, he'd say. He and this cop would know each other by smell, like dogs from the same litter. They'd become good friends.

Mike cruised the lakefront and waited for a call to make a morgue delivery. The coroner's guys claimed they were too busy to bag and haul a body. They'd show up and declare the citizen dead. Mike spent his days tailing them, this dumpy Pakistani from Devon Avenue, and a South Side Irish with blue dog eyes. They were always getting called onward, northwest for a Jordanian custodian who hung himself with a heavy-duty extension cord, up to Argyle Street for a rainy-eyed Cambodian that got stabbed in the neck. They'd make the death pronouncement, then leave, joking about waking up sick from yesterday's tandoori chicken. It's that buffet on Devon, the Irish guy would say. Why do you take me there?

Petersen opened a four-pack of apple bran muffins from a grocery store bakery. He ate fast and the crumbs fell on his lap. He was thin, but he wouldn't be in a year.

"You really have to kick squirrels off an old woman," Petersen said. "The guys talk about it. The old squirrel girl, they say."

"There was a call about some screaming," Mike said. "The neighbor showed me the two-flat, and the door was unlocked. I went up the stairs, and inside, all the windows were open. There were leaves and sticks on the floor and squirrels sitting on the sofa like house cats. The old woman had fallen and broken her hip and the squirrels were just lying on her chest, keeping her warm."

"They bite her?"

"No. I told you. She fell and broke her hip."

"They were wild squirrels."

"The kind that live in trees," Mike said.

"I wouldn't have touched it. That's for animal control."

Pretty soon, Mike would ask Petersen about his softball team, then ignore him while he talked about how their bar sponsor got condemned over one rat. I could see if they found five or six, Petersen would say, but not just one. He'd talk loud, wanting Mike to hear him, vaguely knowing he was like an infomercial you glanced while changing television channels.

They were two blocks away from the first morgue call. It was a corner graystone on Webster with stained-glass windows. The trees between the sidewalk and the curb had lost limbs during the first autumn storm.

Petersen stumbled getting out of the wagon. The guys, used to the squad cars, expected the ground to be closer. Mike stopped laying odds on who was smart enough to remember the drop. The fat cops, the chow-hounds, had a junkie's intelligence that he kept overlooking.

"Mike the Kike lives here," Petersen said.

"What?"

"Mike Rosen. He's a defense lawyer. He takes mopers' money and accepts plea bargains. They know they're getting time, and they pay him to get less. He never steps into a courtroom."

Mike Spence breathed up some rain.

"The guy collects lamps. Real fancy ones. You see them on at night."

"Let's go," Mike said.

In the house, he moved ahead of Petersen, the hallway wet with dirty footprints. Cops loved to walk through puddles and track up oak floors. There were mirrors of different sizes, the frames all painted oak, and in them he saw the detectives lighting their Kools off one Zippo. The mirrored shapes sectioned their bodies into parts while they shared the flame. The Mexican detective had just finished telling a joke. He smiled and nodded like a salesman. Mike listened and came closer, holding his radio.

"Kiss my ass, Ruiz," the black detective said. He wore an olive suit and his head was shaved.

"No," Ruiz said. "The right kind of black guy, a palomino horse, and you got Leroy Rogers."

"I can't see it."

"Roy Rogers as a black guy would be Leroy Rogers. You must accept that for the joke to be funny."

The black detective let out his Kool smoke and blew Ruiz a kiss. He showed him some tongue and the red was foamy in the hall light.

"You and your fag shit," Ruiz said.

Mike walked between the detectives into the room. The tape outlined where Rosen had fallen dead. The body was moved away from the stencil, the feet on their sides, the toes slack. It was dressed like the Viet Cong in the picture lying on the desk, the black shorts, the plaid shirt, and there was a bullet hole through the temple. Mike watched Petersen look between the print and the body, then understand he didn't know what he was seeing. His eyes soon lightened. Petersen had probably resumed thinking about cashing his CDs and day trading small.

Mike started bagging the body alone. His partners never knew his rhythm, and it was easier to leave them looking out the window like Eddie Petersen. The job of getting the bodies inside was like changing a hospital patient's bed with him in it. He also knew the detectives had been waiting for him to take the body to Harrison by the way Ruiz kept looking at his silver Rolex.

"You guys stop for blow jobs?" Ruiz said.

The detective had only been a face from crime scenes until the black detective spoke his name, some squat, loud guy. Petersen was looking out the window like he could see a girl.

"They sweep for prints?" Mike said.

"Why would I let you in here if they hadn't swept for prints," Ruiz said.

"They left the picture," Mike said. He pointed at the dying Viet Cong, and wondered if the guy was already dead when Eddie Adams snapped the camera.

The black detective looked off down the hallway, chewing on a toothpick. Ruiz packed his Kool against his Zippo. He was like an arrogant track coach, his eyes full-wire.

"You see smoke coming out of the picture?" Ruiz said.

Mike saw the body, the bare feet, before the print. "No," he said.

"Then the picture didn't kill him."

Mike looked at the blood on the ceiling near where the bullet hit. It was like fresh paint.

"The body's dressed like the Viet Cong getting shot," Mike said.

Ruiz walked over and put the picture in his pocket.

"Rosen brought home sixteen-year-old black girls from Cabrini Green," Ruiz said to his partner. "He'd sodomize them, then buy ribs and champagne."

"I bet it was a parolee who shot him," the partner said. "One pissed-off spic just off ten years fed time."

"Rosen robs these kids. They'd get the same sentence with a public defender."

"I bet it was a pissed-off spic."

"One of those girls did this," Ruiz said.

"No. She'd want to keep the deal. Your nephew Javier shot him."

"You wouldn't give a Mexican your old toothbrush."

"Javier would just scratch it against the curb until he had a knife."

"No," Ruiz said. "He'd thank you from deep. Not all of us chicken flickers are killers."

Mike zipped the bag shut and watched Petersen step closer to the window as if the glass was an open door. Then he saw that Rosen had changed before he died. His clothes, tan Angel Flight's and a blue silk shirt, lay in the corner, not even boxed off by the tape.

There were creases in the picture where the killer held it and just stared. Mike imagined his eyes stinging from not blinking while his thumb dented the print. This guy was beyond writing novels. He understood that reading was too much effort for a city that frequented bookstore cafés. He wanted the innocent to know what some men must do so that others can sleep well, and if the sleepers keep ordering more protection, they should understand what happens in the dark. Dressing a defense attorney who never went to Vietnam like the pistol-shot Viet Cong, then staging the execution exactly, showed a killer who wanted the sleepers to feel what orders meant. They must experience being trapped in a lethal violence they cannot escape.

Mike stood nodding. He thought about the man staring at the picture, and wondered if he realized the detectives were throwing away his work like bored insurance secretaries do auto claims. He tried not to smile.

13

Goetzler walked Webster, from the pole lamps outside DePaul's rectory to slanting Clybourn Street where the buses headed northwest into the lake wind, filled with the babushkas who clean these condos, the Mexicans who bag the gutter leaves.

He held an umbrella and a cell phone so he'd see the green screen blink BLOCKED when Nick called back about Annie. Goetzler had rung three times since noon, and the same electronic man spoke on the voice mail, indicating to only leave numeric messages. He'll call, Goetzler told himself, these people always need money.

Last night, Mike Rosen undid his belt and his fly before he walked into the office. In the dark, Goetzler saw the rain smears on his own glasses. Rosen looked at the floor and made sure not to step on the white rugs. He hit a switch and ten Tiffany lamps lit. Goetzler never noticed the light switch, and guessed the lamps were there for the Polksa in black stockings to dust on Wednesday nights while Rosen watched from behind this desk.

Goetzler saw spots. He blinked his eyes hard. Rosen was a dark shape moving quickly.

He never considered a light switch. The thing was ruined.

When the dots became smears, Goetzler fired the silenced pistol, still blinking his eyes when the body fell. It sounded like a fat man stepping from bed. He couldn't see and forgot he held the .38 for a long minute.

He never meant to kill him. He'd only wanted Rosen to change clothes, then show him the picture, asking him if he got the joke. Do you see the connection, he'd say. But Goetzler wore a William Westmoreland mask, the eyeholes cut big. Rosen wouldn't remember him anyway, but he would know the picture, and he might recall the photographer's name. He could have an opinion about how it ended the American Century; some University of Illinois poly-sci reel about how Vietnam was the direct result of . . . Goetzler would explain the your side, my side irony of the picture, the cops versus the not-cops, and then ask him why he didn't understand more quickly. You made three million by getting cops mad in court, he'd say while Rosen looked for an answer. You should know what this is about. In the picture, you are on the dead guy's side.

It took Goetzler ten minutes to dress the body. But he felt giddy, even pleased with himself. Kerm would see Goetzler as Kerm, and if Annie could know he shot Rosen, the odds were short that she'd see him for nothing.

The light at Barnes and Noble was white as paper. Goetzler held a book, *The Autobiography of U. S. Grant*, open to the Shiloh pages, and imagined the general bourbon drunk and tied to his horse. He was a failure at thirty-four. Goetzler loved a second-chance story, and Grant was the phoenix.

He watched the blond girls in the café cram for the GMAT. He stared until they blurred with their books, their fingers wound in ponytails, and imagined himself in a restaurant bar filled with Weber Industrial Supply management, a trattoria on the Gold Coast, some subtle place on a loud street. Goetzler would force the general president into conversation by paying with fifties. He'd count the money out, an inch of bills folded in half. Grant was a sot, Goetzler would say, pointing at the thick-faced portrait, but the man never got lost. He killed to keep hold—Indians, Mexicans, the whole of the Confederate Army—because he remembered being a failure who counted cow hides for his little brother. He made himself indispensable to more powerful men. He even wrote his autobiography when he was dying of throat cancer, all to keep his family in money. The MBAs would become quiet and look at Goetzler without half watching ESPN on the television. They'd want to know more about Grant's story, and never once look back at Sports Center while Goetzler talked. You really got a handle on where to find leadership lessons, they'd say. Can you jockey that into a team building exercise?

He stood among the books and dreamed of giving the management seminar on Grant. The suits would be sitting along three tables in the blue room of white noise, and he'd be explaining Shiloh. He wouldn't talk about how the dead were white with peach blossoms knocked from the trees by the rifle fire. The guys would write that down and ask him during the break what the flower petals had to do with anything. They'd be interested in the way Grant got water and gunpowder to the lines and all the steps in that process. In the end, he also knew they wouldn't care about the formations of the battle, or how Grant was lucky enough to have his greatest Confederate adversary, General Albert Sidney Johnson, get killed on Shiloh's first day. They'd want to know how Grant approached the subject of evaluation with his senior staff officers.

He put the book down and walked to the chairs before the podium. People were sitting and waiting for ex-Rainman Will Avers to give his *Tribune* advertised reading—aging men with ponytails and liver-spotted baldness, gray women wearing the residue from too many bead fairs. Like Goetzler, they wanted to see the sixties radical with earrings in both ears and a real neat goatee smeared black by Just for Men. He was ten minutes late. Goetzler quit looking at his watch when he noticed nobody else was doing it.

Avers had written a book about being a fugitive from the federal government for thirteen years. Goetzler read it in this store, beneath this hard light. Avers claimed Manson knew shit from shinola. You got to kill the pigs, he joked about once saying. He made bombs, taught black kids on the West Side how to sing and hold hands, met with the Viet Cong in Canada, got implicated in a conspiracy after blowing up two ROTC offices, Madison and Iowa City, then went underground and swapped women like baseball cards until his father's lawyer cut a deal with the FBI. He took a Ph.D. in history. He got an NEH fellowship to study the effects of Reaganomics on urban school reform, but instead wrote a memoir of his time on the lam. His publisher advanced him. He bought a three-bedroom condo in Lincoln Park, the lake and the maple trees beyond bay windows, granite countertops, a hot tub with jets that could dent car doors. He had parties for his graduate students. He was heavy into yoga and went to a place in Ravenswood and cruised divorced schoolteachers. He gave interviews on local NPR, plug for the book, and they treated him like the Left's Audie Murphy. If I had the stuff, I'd be you, they almost said.

In person, he was a skinny guy who smiled like a game show host. A girl in vegan shoes introduced him, reading a pull quote from a review, "Avers thoughtfully resists the pitfalls of nostalgia." He scratched the die off his goatee, watching the flecks fall upon his book pages like crumbs. He spoke without using a microphone, telling about the night he waited by a highway-side pay phone for a call that didn't come, and how it took three days before he knew the caller was blown up making a bomb. The people were smiling and nodding as if they'd waited for the same kind of call. Avers paused often for water, and his hands just fit around the bottle, his fingers small for his height. When the Evian emptied, he looked unstrung until he found another bottle, then did a perfect imitation of Johnny Cash.

"I thought I was going to have to drink the runoff from Luther's boots."

The people laughed, even the ones who didn't know what he was talking about. Avers owned the imitation. He'd thought to swallow his words like Cash did, because at Folsom Prison, Cash played nine songs before asking for a drink, but the water was slow in coming, and Cash thought his bass player's sweaty boots might do. Goetzler knew all about this record because his first sergeant in Germany, a black guy from Toledo, loved Johnny Cash, and eyeballed people who thought it was funny.

Avers took off his glasses. He'd gotten bright in the eyes.

"You learn these things after hiding in people's basements for thirteen years," he said. "You should hear my Liza Minnelli. But Cash's song 'The Man in Black' kept me going through it all. Like Johnny said, 'I couldn't put a rainbow on my back and pretend that everything's just fine.' "

There were second acts, but the men who stayed believers were the ones who never lost everything. Neither Goetzler nor Avers were such men. Goetzler figured Avers's time underground in the white noise of basement bedrooms, having running-without-moving dreams set in penitentiary mess halls, taught him that believers got paid the same as shirkers. He decided that if he could ever walk as himself, he'd write his Ph.D. and get a pension. He'd turn their kids. The academic left, once those string-haired grad students in black berets and leather jackets, figured it owed Avers, and he did, too. After the police department, Goetzler tried doing the same thing at Weber. He fought for capitalism and now the corporations must make a place.

Will Avers would be the little girl running from napalm. Kim Luc Phu, *the girl in the picture,* her arms forever dangling while her burning village boiled paddy water. Goetzler wanted to make Avers understand that he was protecting the little girls from both the Viet Cong and the South Vietnamese soldiers, not napalming them. He entertained notions of getting a camcorder and sending the tape to Fox News Chicago. He could even burn CDs and put Avers running naked through an alley on the Internet. But, first, he'd blindfold him with duct tape and then tape a lamented picture of Kim Luc Phu around his neck. He'd send Avers into the traffic on Halsted Street and get the whole thing on camcorder. Yahoo might even file the story under news of the weird because Avers's backside was sure to be among the whitest ever spotted.

14

Annie stood in the Motel 6 room and looked at the parked cars on Ohio Street, waiting for the date's knock. She wore a robe over black lingerie for hotel day calls, and wondered why these men spent five hundred dollars for an hour of kissless sex with her. Catholic brunettes from Hoffman Estates got naked for carry-out sushi and *St. Elmo's Fire* on DVD, and they kissed with their tongues.

But these johns couldn't score with women who only wanted a date for Christmas Day at their parents' house.

She believed they were all low-hanging fruit. They came on the hour, some tubby and apologetic, some health-club sleek and lying about themselves. The cop was a better class of john, though maybe a john the same. She'd watch him before deciding, but the rest were mostly from the bottom of the world.

When the knock came, she opened the door, and her date was a crew-cut Italian mix. He'd wrestled in high school, but didn't have the guts for the Marine Corps, so the haircut remained part of the old fantasy. They were always dreamers.

He looked at Annie and chewed with an open mouth. After he came inside, she pressed his eyes. They were like painted glass.

"I can taste you already," he said.

Annie's eyes watered from his Aramis.

He took Velcro restraints from his leather coat and held them out for her with one hand.

"I don't do that," she said.

The guy smiled, tossed her restraints, which she let fall, and then threw his patrolman's star on the bed. She went cold like the windows. He was a tactical cop, a uniform who gets to wear blue jeans and a bulletproof vest and put kids over cruiser hoods for selling joints. He was small, but still a problem. She bent over and picked up the restraints.

"Leave the lingerie on," he said, "then lay on your stomach."

She took off her robe and turned for the bed. The spread lay on the floor from the Loyola kid at noon.

"I'll give you the tip later," the cop said. "I'll be sure to tell you to work hard and save your money."

When she lay down, she put the restraints beside her, then buried her face between the pillows while the Velcro tore. He soon started on her ankles.

The next day, Annie stayed in the apartment. She tried yoga twice, but shook and lost balance doing the plank. She sat in panties and a T-shirt, hallucinating the cotton weighed heavy, and calmed herself by looking at the cop's blinded window. He wasn't home.

The agency had been calling all afternoon. She held the phone and watched the BLOCKED light, wondering how far she could push Goetzler. Yesterday, she hadn't seen a cop in that john, and she was getting scared. She liked the tidy arrangement with Goetzler since he wanted absolution for Vietnam and not sex. For love, there was the cop across the street. She'd keep giving Goetzler silence and he'd busy himself by taking it as a challenge.

But she might answer her cell next time. Nick would offer her another five percent, maybe ten for anything over two hours. After it got dark, the cop went running so she turned her phone off. Nick went to pieces if he slept on things. He'd give her fifteen percent by noon tomorrow.

Annie turned from the window, looking for a cat, but they were hiding. When her hands started running across the floorboards, she decided to wear an *ao dai*, and meet the cop after his run. She got dressed inside two minutes, smiling about the white silk on her back, and watched herself in the mirror. She acted shy and nodded, touching her hips with curled fingers.

She went downstairs and stood in the side-street wind and let her cheeks get wet. She'd even turned and checked herself in the door glass, the silk train blowing up and twisting. The cop's apartment was lit, one lamp by the chair. The rain hit the bell she'd ring.

In Chicago, in this sideways rain, Annie made the wind warm and put herself in Hue's pine air near the Perfume River where it passed beneath the Thoung Tu Bridge. Her uncle had been killed there in 1968, and every day her father pointed out the stretch of pavement. A nice boy, her father said of him. He liked pears and taught himself French. That woman of his, he told Annie. It was her pussy that turned him into a VC. No hair, he'd say to me. Like a girl's. Sometimes, Annie would stand alone where her uncle died, shot by U.S. Marines, and try imagining a pear while the cyclos hauled live catfish in barrels off to where Le Loi Street turned into trees.

She'd seen no pictures of pears, but she guessed they looked like mangoes. Sometimes, she'd be eating this pear, but knowing it was a mango, when the schoolgirls started home from the university, their white *ao dais* like all *ao dais*, covering everything and hiding nothing. She forgot the fruit and her dead uncle and decided the white silk allowed those girls to fly like egrets or nightingales, and if she wore it, she'd learn to fly by next week. She was still too young for the *ao dai*, and had even left Vietnam in black cotton pajamas. Her mother always threatened not to make one for her. Keep sleeping with those cats, she'd say. The time will come for your *ao dai* and you'll still be dressed like a little girl.

Tonight, in this wind-dreamed-warm, Annie wasn't happy she'd learned the difference between Bosc and Anjou pears. She also hated knowing that an *ao dai* cost only fifty dollars on Argyle Street.

She walked between the cars and crossed the street to the cop's. The puddles were sleeved by wet leaves. That night, she'd sat with her back to the window, and knew he'd returned from his run when his desk lamp lit in her television screen. She couldn't look to see if he was home. When she did, even glancing away quickly, she'd see him move across the window. She'd try making him vague, then a shadow against the curb, but her lips had tasted the salt of him, and he'd smelled like he did in her dreams, alkaline and hard soap.

When Annie saw herself in his door glass, her arm was long, and the rain flecked her *ao dai*. The wet silk turned dark, like wiped ashes. She tried drying a mark with her finger, rubbing until the dark color diluted. She touched the bell, using her free hand. The spot wouldn't fade. She was only pushing the darkness through the fibers.

15

Mike's first quarters went through the squad-room coffee machine. Then, trying again, the coins stuck, and he hit the return
lever. He pushed down hard while Detective Manny "Rim-Job"
Ruiz was making Lieutenant Rossi believe that a moper killed
Rosen. They stood in the cold light thronged through the squad-
room windows, two detectives in altered suits from T.J.Maxx, the
dirt from the panes shadowed upon their faces. For Ruiz, the
story went like this:

A Willie went away for ten years after getting caught with two
kilos, but paid Rosen his last thirty grand to get the sentence reduced to three. Rosen could have pled for five, but took it to trial.
They offer half, Willie had said, you know they don't got any big
shit. Willie spent the 1990s talking jailhouse smack about how he
would eat Mike the Kike's fingers like rib tips. But Willie got into
a fight with a guard his third week and broke the man's jaw with a
wood-shop hammer. His twenty-fourth day inside had already determined he would not make parole (a hope he carried like Allah
through two hearings after becoming Muhammad Kareem Said in
a late night conversion). He wound up at a halfway house on the

West Side and sat through mandatory Narcotics Anonymous meetings because heroin had softened his incarceration after he burned the Koran in his cell toilet. He got clean and then broke in and shot Rosen in the head.

"You know how Rosen operated," Ruiz said.

Rossi nodded like a tollbooth worker. Some days, depending on the suit, he looked more thin than fat.

"Your report has a beginning, a middle, and an end," he said. "I like that."

"I keep my stuff tight," Ruiz said.

"Sure, Manny," Rossi said. "You're tighter than a bus at rush hour."

"I pride myself, LT."

"Sure you do."

"I do everything like Mexico is watching. It's the same way Sammy Sosa feels about the Dominican Republic. We're role models for our people."

"Great," Rossi said. "Just keep your off-duty guys from wearing their guns into bars. Downtown is going to start suspending without pay."

Mike Spence drank the machine coffee. He knew Ruiz never worked a case he couldn't solve without cruising Borders and mindsexing the blond mothers. Rossi also knew and showed it by the way he bent his lips into a smile. Next month, the lieutenant was starting a parks and recreation assignment where he'd announce police league fights at St. Andrews. He was waiting for the Grand Avenue Italian who could beat a West Side black. I'll see it before I die, he'd say. The guy loved watching teenagers fight and the movie Indians die.

The ballistics report confirmed a .38 bullet killed Rosen. The gun had a short barrel, like the piece from the picture. Nobody spoke about how Rosen was dressed as the dying Viet Cong because Ruiz didn't understand it and feared being removed from a case. He had his scenario. He claimed any killer's true motives came to him with his morning cigarette, the day after the murder, though he always used the same story, and substituted Willie for Hector when necessary. Crime Scene was still deciding how the shooter got inside; the entry and exit was clean. Willie would have been madder than this, Mike thought, he would have busted up the lamps before shooting Rosen. But nobody wanted Mike's opinion, even if they knew how Ruiz's investigations always went: he'd round up some of Rosen's recently incarcerated clients, then sweat them, and come up with nothing. Lieutenant Sally Rossi wouldn't let the investigation stay warm for more than a month—a cold case got filed in the drawer beneath the solved ones. The only people who would miss Rosen were the antique dealers and some gay shoe salesman on Oak Street.

Mike knew the killer was invisible in the city. He was alone, but not by choice, an arrogant man who needed to have ideas of himself, associations with history, dreams of riding the steppes with Cossacks while the wind split the high grass and the slain Ottomans went to the fallen shucks. The picture meant everything. The killer used it to say that he'd been interrupted by Vietnam, and didn't know it for thirty years. He was angry over sitting too long in tropical heat while other men, his peers, stayed cool in Rush Street jazz lounges, sipping manhattans with red-headed perfume-tester girls from Marshall Fields, while Americans walked on the moon and General Giap told the BBC that the Vietnamese people would offer a million more lives for national liberation.

Mike walked down the hall when Ruiz started with his blond jokes and Lieutenant Rossi looked out the window, his head more bald than last month. Mike only drove the wagon, and if there was no morgue call, they made him set up the no-left-turn signs along Ashland Avenue fifteen minutes before rush hour.

Mike Spence went out into the sunny cold, this duty morning, and realized that he was the only uniform who still wore the hat. Now, Susan and Rosen were the same: just dead, their cases filed in metal drawers where mice with tough teeth had burrowed inside and shat in the folders. He didn't know how long he should care about either one.

That night, Mike sat breathing hard after his run. He'd done six miles in thirty-six minutes, and ran wishing the woman would be lying over a car hood when he returned to Claremont Street. He stretched his legs and hoped the rain would warm. But she was not on a car, and her window was dark. Even after he showered with Zest, his mind still wouldn't quiet. This woman could be like a joint.

The apartment seemed to grow smaller, the doors shrinking, the windows fading into squares. He felt unwired because he understood why the killer left the pictures, and thinking about it kept his lungs from slowing. This guy showed people, but he was sad and pathetic to think murder could make a difference. He'd probably lived his life plotting this revenge, and he'd wasted many good hours. Mike guessed he surprised himself by actually killing Mike Rosen.

But General Loan shooting the VC was the perfect image. Mike couldn't do that with a hundred novels. Too bad the cops watched more ESPN than History Channel and couldn't get the gag.

Mike fantasized *60 Minutes* running the story. He'd be talking to Steve Croft, happy with the man's football coach cynicism, himself already promoted to homicide detective. Steve Croft would see the killer as a man who lived in the past too long, and tried to dialogue with the protected world, using the pictures because he'd never been able to stop thinking about the ways they affected his idea of Vietnam being purposeful. Having reported from Bien Hoa during the war, Croft would know how history had made this guy.

He and Croft would make some points together. Afterward, he saw himself telling Kenjuan Mills where to go smile and lick. He'd carry the gold homicide shield, and Mills might become a property crimes detective. But, in the end, the *60 Minutes* story would be sandwiched between an exposé on why the U.S. Government spends fifty bucks for a six-dollar hammer, and a profile of a young soprano who makes Met audiences speak in tongues.

Mike then called Dilger without thinking about it. Like Croft, his old friend would understand what the murderer was doing. He dialed 411, said Edward Dilger, Burkburnett, Texas, and the operator connected him for no extra charge. Inside a minute, Dilger was drawling hello, and before Mike responded, he imagined a house trailer with an oil pump in the backyard and lots of white-hazy sky.

"Dilger," Mike said into the phone, "it's Spence."

"God dog."

"You still sucking air, sunshine?"

"I'm tougher than the guy you named me after in your book," Dilger said back. "I never regretted trying to break up Chopper and Bozak that night, but the consequences were hard."

"I needed a moral center," Mike said.

"What?"

"You were the sensitive guy among those shaven-headed maniacs."

"No, Spence," Dilger said. "That was you."

His old friend sounded good, but Mike dismissed Dilger's peace as the result of hitting the twelfth "get-real" step in AA. The oil derrick was still pumping in the backyard.

"I got something to tell you," Mike said.

"You still a writer?"

"I'm a cop now."

"You sucked as a soldier. But now you get to lie without all the hard work of writing."

Mike figured Dilger was sober. All the better if AA did it.

He told him about the killer and the picture. He spoke plainly and Dilger listened without interruption. Mike then told him about the woman posing in her window and how she waited for him one night, lying on wet leaves, but he left out Susan's death. Dilger didn't know about her, and Mike didn't know how to start. But the hooker felt like a long nap. He made sure his old friend knew that.

"Play with the hooker," Dilger told him, "but forget the picture. It's about Iraq now. Here in North Texas, people want to win this coming war. Vietnam is not on their minds."

"But they are repeating a war."

"Who wants to be reminded of a mistake when you're wanting to win."

Mike pushed the receiver into his mouth.

"Every war repeats a war, Spence," Dilger said. "It's how we understand them."

Mike listened while Dilger spat Copenhagen into a Coke can. The motion would be the same: Dilger leaning to his left and shooting the dark spit from the side of his mouth, but Mike couldn't imagine his face having any trace of the soldier boy who scored with Georgetown girls. After the army, Dilger moved to

Florida and listened only to Metallica, and started using speed instead of running in the morning. Inside two years, Dilger had lost it.

"One Jiffy Lube is a pain in the neck," Dilger said. "But four pay."

"You running Jiffy Lubes?"

"People are getting too fat to change their own oil, Spence. It's easy money. Most Americans can't fit under their cars."

"How'd you get started with that?"

"A lawyer got my discharge fixed," he said. "The next day, I applied for a VA small business loan and took some accounting courses at the junior college."

"I always guessed you liked lube on your hands," Mike said.

"You don't get it, Spence. I own the Jiffy Lubes. I only changed oil in the franchisee training course. Are you still getting paid for telling lies?"

"That's why I should look into the picture. I could figure this out."

"I thought you liked the killer. You said the killer is speaking for us. He saw men fall and burn when nobody really cared."

"I could find him. These detectives don't understand the crime scene. I'd be set in the department."

"You ever quit?"

Mike Spence said nothing and held the receiver. Edward Dilger was fine. Mike had been wrong these years.

"Get a VA business loan," Dilger said. "Figure out what to sell. In the end, it's only you caring about this bullshit."

"It happened to you, Dilge. The MPs beat you for nothing while frat boys did beer bongs."

"That's why I can say the future amputees coming home from Iraq aren't going to listen about Vietnam or care about frat boys.

You have to realize the inevitability of things or you'll never move on."

"Why did we have to watch men fall on fire. You remember wanting to get them, and not knowing how."

"We could have stayed home and worked at Kmart, then figured out how to get promoted."

"You didn't do that."

"You didn't either."

Mike jumped when the buzzer sounded. He tried looking out the window, but couldn't see the street from where he sat.

"Is that your door?" Dilger said.

"It's nothing."

"I have to split anyway. I'm going fishing in Peru with my son and I have to enter some receipts into QuickBooks."

The buzzer went again.

"You better get that," Dilger said. "Keep in touch, Spence."

When the dial tone sounded, Mike hung up the phone and headed for the door and the stairs. Dilger had never taken his number. Mike also hated Dilger for not wanting to tell the old stories anymore.

Mike saw white wings through his door window until he understood the wings were the blowing panels from the woman's dress. She was small and the gusts hit her, but she didn't move. She kept her arms straight along her waist while the wind played in the silk. Her eyes were quiet tonight, not loud like they were on the leaves.

Schoolgirls and fiancées wore the *ao dai*. The dress was for virgins, the girls who sell orchids from baskets. He'd found out after a Google search.

He walked for the door laughing over her stunt.

Maybe she was the killer, this woman with chameleonlike eye

energy, and she was avenging what the United States let North Vietnam do to Saigon after April 1975. She watched priests shot in their sanctuaries, schoolteachers raped and sent to reeducation camps, and her mother trade family jade, piece by piece, for dirty rice. Her father could have been a South Vietnamese army major, her uncle a Viet Cong sapper. The war may have erased her entire childhood.

But he laughed once more before he walked outside and she came warm and unsmiling into his arms. They had not met eyes very long. He was sure this woman made too much money to even consider revenge. In the wind, her *ao dai* panels twisted around his waist and he floated when her wet lips brushed his own. If she was mad about having been a boat person, she wasn't anymore.

16

Goetzler read the brief in the *Tribune*'s Metro section about Rosen being murdered. The police department didn't have a suspect, or a motive. The blurb went three lines, the space mostly taken by Rosen's age and address. The reporter said nothing about the picture, and how the deceased's clothes were identical to the executed Viet Cong's. Goetzler then read the *Tribune* all week, mornings in the sauna, while caffeinated firemen, just off their shifts, poured water on the rocks and the steam made the newsprint run. There was nothing.

Tonight, he was driving to tell Annie what he'd done for her. He'd say it without saying it, the way he'd been practicing for three days.

You know, he told his reflection in the car window. They are smug because they said we'd fail in Vietnam.

After listening about the murder, Annie's eyes almost cat quiet, she might tell him that his soldiering in Vietnam was humane and made a horrible situation bearable. You protected me from both sides, she'd tell him.

But Goetzler figured Annie would only look at him, and not

being on the clock, refuse to recognize him. He'd simply confront her and explain what happened to Mike Rosen and remind her why it was a victory for them. He wanted her to hear, and remind her she was Vietnamese. He might jar her enough to remember what a small-town school district had defined away. This might be his chance to find her for real.

I watched good men die for your people, he'd tell her. You should love them with an open heart.

Goetzler had discovered that she rented in a three-flat a mile west of Wrigley Field. He also knew the cars that drove her to the dates, a black BMW and a blue Jeep Cherokee. One night, he'd waited in the elevator, keeping the door open, and watched her driver pull up. He then jumped back inside, after holding the elevator for himself, and went to the twenty-sixth floor. He also knew that Nick only serviced this neighborhood, and Annie worked Tuesdays and Thursdays. For a week, he drove between Lake Shore Drive and Sheridan, and waited to see the agency cars pulling out of high-rise roundabouts with her inside. It took him two Thursday nights, but he finally spotted Annie in the blue Jeep, driven by a grayed Italian in a leather jacket. He followed her home. The driver was too stupid to sense Goetzler's tail. He was talking and looking at Annie in the rearview mirror.

She lived on Claremont, a long street of maples. Goetzler drove and looked for her number, 3329. Two three-flats had white Christmas lights wound about the locked wrought iron. He couldn't imagine her among the sports bars and supermarkets and the coin-op Laundromats where new MBAs washed their Kellogg Business School running shorts among the last of the Mexicans. These were the cracked sidewalks she took to get a mocha latte and crumble berry cake. She wore sweatpants, and a baseball cap with her ponytail yanked through the size adjuster. He was sure she walked a dog and looked nothing like herself.

Across from Annie's two-flat, Goetzler saw the panels of a white *ao dai* circle a man's waist before he realized it was Annie hugging a man. He pulled his Jeep to the curb while the man lifted his wet socks from the concrete, stepped backward. He stopped when he felt Annie's body give to him. The rain had formed the silk to her legs like hose. The man faced the door and held her, pulling their stomachs together. Annie was laughing while the rain disappeared into her forehead.

When Goetzler stepped from his Jeep, not knowing what he'd do with this man, Annie saw him immediately and smiled when they met eyes. She kissed at Goetzler from around the man's head, but her unblinking stare told him that if he went any closer, she'd someday kill him with a hairpin.

Goetzler looked at the Jeep key in his small hand, and Annie didn't blink until he returned to his driver's seat. He drove away, wishing he'd not tried this, and thought himself stupid for opening the door.

With the man, Goetzler had seen Annie as a girl-*sanh* stooped outside Tan San Nhut selling orchids, but after Annie spotted Goetzler, she transformed into the madam of a Cholon whorehouse filled with Cav Scouts in Saigon for twenty-four hours. Like the madams, she'd kill you with a cracked porcelain vase while you slept.

Looking at her with the man, a stunned athletic guy in stocking feet, Goetzler remembered Saigon and how the Cav Scouts slapped his shiny MP helmet liner, and laughed at his small hands in white MP gloves. He and Olszewski were always called to the grafted brothels to break up fights. The madam's payment required an officer and senior NCO to always respond, not two baton-happy private first classes with a hundred days left in Vietnam.

We fight the gooks, the Cav Scouts would say, and the MPs fight us.

But Sergeant Olszewski always saved Goetzler. There's a fucking officer center, he'd tell these surly grunts in from Tay Ninh. Goetzler would walk quickly among them while they laughed at his fogged glasses, claiming the defroster off a '60 Impala couldn't dry those specs. He never remembered the Cav Scouts treating him differently, even after he started wearing longer white gloves to enlarge his hands.

17

Annie looked in the cop's shower and imagined his woman's shampoo bottles. She would have the two Suave conditioners afforded a cop's wife, down from the six of her late twenties when she'd had her own place. He'd gotten towels since she left; the cotton felt stiff. She could see where he'd taken down a medicine cabinet. There was no mirror in the bathroom and she laughed because some nights she'd watched him stare into the window glass.

His apartment reminded her of the bare trees when he first walked her backward through the door. He'd taken the pictures from the walls. She'd seen them from across the street, reflecting the ceiling light, then one night, the room was never lit again. He stacked his books off the shelves, like pallets of bricks, and left the shelves in the alley. She saw a different title each time she'd look: *The Sound and the Fury, Slouching Towards Bethlehem, Suttree, Beyond Good and Evil.* He covered his wife's scent by cleaning with pine oil and Comet. He had no dresser and his clothes were folded and piled in the closet. She only remained in the light blue paint on the bedroom walls.

Annie stood naked over the toilet and listened for him to take the fourth step away from the bed. She could pinpoint men in their apartments by counting their steps. She had nightmares about a date corning hard and sudden into a hotel bathroom door, where behind, she was losing her cell phone to a wind that burst through the walls. But the cop moved steady, like streams or merging traffic.

When she went back to his room, the walls were still blue, even in the darkness. He lay beneath blankets, upon his side, and stared at his shadow made by the streetlight. Annie stood in the window and her shadow crossed his own. He didn't move.

Before he'd first kissed her, he parted her lips with his finger. He then took her top lip between his own and she saw herself twinned in his green-black eyes. She became the love beneath him, and he touched his face many times with her wet hair. She looked at him while he'd separate the strands and lay them splayed in his hand before bringing them to his mouth. He never turned away from her.

Now, when Annie got into bed, she couldn't tell if he was sleeping. She listened for air in his nose, but the night was too loud, and she then lay touching the parts of him that made her jealous: the tight skin over his hip bones, the muscle in his shoulders, the eyes that could look away. Then, she discovered that his lids were open.

She thought the cop would speak, but he didn't. He was beyond the window, again. She'd made love to his wishes, but not to him. She drew a line down his back, her finger riding the notches in his spine.

"Your wife watched me first through the window," she said.

He was still as sticks. Annie knew the quiet ones had the brains to destroy themselves.

"Then she left you," she said.

"My wife was killed."

"How?"

She touched his wet neck with her lips. He tasted of the city grass and her own mouth.

"Last summer," he said. "She was the woman killed in the alley."

Annie didn't know there was a woman murdered across the street. She'd been working afternoons and nights during the summer, doing out-calls to Glencoe.

"You wanted to tell me something else," she said.

"She's just dead," he said. "Nobody knows anything more. I think it was a gang initiation. They never took a thing."

"They never found a fingerprint?" she said.

"They looked hard," he said. "It took them a week. I was directing traffic downtown during rush hour."

He lay on his side. The streetlight cast their shadow against the wall, her hand lost in his shoulder, and she wondered what about it he saw. The fingers from the hand that hung from the bed, or the way the streetlight fogged the night.

"You are loyal to your old wishes about your marriage," she said.

"I was just with you," he said.

"Now," she said, "you are with her."

"This is her bed."

"Do you want to meet like this?" she said. "Then go back to the windows."

"No," he said.

"Why don't you look at me?"

"I can't see you and think," he said.

The cop went quiet, but he didn't ask her to leave. With a woman, he was like a car that slid into a ditch over a trick turn.

He probably couldn't say how he ended up kissing their stomachs five minutes after thinking they were bored and wanting to go home. He had his own reality, but merely reacted in this world. She put her ear to his back. Men like him took air the way they attempted canyon turns.

In college, Annie worked for the Hilton and Towers on South Michigan Avenue. She kept track of the safety deposit room where old men locked five Rolexes into a box, then walked out like penguins. She answered the phones in the call center and connected throaty women to the rooms of conventioning oncologists. She worked the checkout desk, smiled in her blue Hilton skirt and blazer, but the people complained that they couldn't understand her, even though the bill always totaled. They'd tell the manager how her voice was muted by the lobby's acoustics. There's too much open air. Within a day, she was assisting the concierge, a gay man named Ron, and telling grayed couples that the Berghoff was the best restaurant south of Lake Street. The spaetzle is something to have, she'd say, working on speaking louder. The couples waited for this advice in short lines while Ron cleaned his black horn-rim glasses.

"They herd like the elk on the Discovery Channel," he'd say of the couples. "Just disgusting."

Ron wore a string tie with his Hilton blazer. They left him alone about it because he'd helped a Mexican lady, a towel folder in the fitness center, file a sexual harassment complaint at federal court. The day Annie first met him, the sky looked warm, blue traced with yellow, but it was not. He pointed at his tie, then the glasses.

"People really take me for Elvis Costello," he said.

Annie didn't know what he was talking about. Ron put himself farther into her eyes. She felt stuck beside him on a long flight, jammed between his soft legs and the window. There were ten pounds around his waist that he couldn't lose by jogging.

"I can't have a drink south of Houston without getting hassled," he said. "Last time, this woman wouldn't leave it alone. She was a bridge and tunnel person."

He stopped and looked sideways at Annie.

"You don't know what the hell I'm talking about," he said.

Annie shook her head. In a minute, she would not hear him. His mouth could move, but there'd be no volume. She first needed the sky a certain way—bare and blue for ten seconds. She looked out the glass doors, but traffic was stopped.

"I'm talking about New York," Ron said. "The bridge and tunnel people live in New Jersey—they come over to ruin the air. Elvis Costello is a famous singer."

Annie couldn't see across the street. The Channel Two news team was splattered with mud on the side of a bus. The people walking the sidewalk reminded her of snapshots spilled from a box.

"Are you from New York?" she said.

"No," Ron said. "But my soul is."

"You've never lived there?"

"No," he said. "I've just spent a lot of time."

There was a young Galway bar back named Jack working the phony Irish pub across the lobby. There were harpists on Wednesday nights, heavyset guys who only smiled when they played. Annie and Ron watched him dry pint glasses. He'd create resistance with the towel, making his forearms strain. All afternoon he did things like that—pressing his hands into the bar, or standing straight and squaring his shoulders. He had red hair, short over his ears, and

Annie imagined he'd look younger while he slept. The first time he looked at her, she thought of keys being thrown across the room.

His eyes are like rocks beneath water, Ron said.

The concierge started winking and waving at Jack. He'd go to the bar and tilt his head, smiling, before slowing his voice to ask for a glass of water with lime. Jack put his hands in his pockets and looked at his shoes. Maybe he's trying to go away, she thought, and he can't see outside.

Ron grinned at Annie whenever Jack went to the men's room. He'd walk from behind the concierge desk and pass the gold elevators. Annie imagined them standing at the sinks: Jack trying to not see Ron in the mirror while Ron kept looking for his eyes. Jack left without buttoning his shirt cuffs. He put on his watch behind the bar. Ron smelled like cigarettes when he came back to the desk.

"Why should you get off and not me?" he'd say.

She stared out the window. Today, the sky was blue enough to take her, even if it was cold white above the lake, but the street never cleared of traffic. She needed a straight gaze without pigeons and people, then ten seconds alone with the sky. She waited for the stoplight and hoped the flocks in Grant Park had already sprung.

One night, Jack kept sending glasses of water to Ron. The lime twists were already squeezed. Ron waved at Jack, then drank the water quickly, sending the glass back with the waitress. His face was too tight for his lips to bend, but he still smiled and looked sideways at Jack. The bartender waved like men do for drinks at busy nightclubs. When Ron went to the men's room, bloated with cold water, Jack ran across the lobby. His haircut was recent.

"I had to get rid of the wanker to ask you something," he said.

She felt herself blinking. He smelled of snuck Marlboros. Annie saw the red box through his shirt pocket.

"Would you like to go dancing?" he said.

She watched a cigarette smolder in the ashtray between the elevators. Jack looked right at her and talked.

"There's some good clubs if you aren't afraid of the blacks," he said. "But they're fine with me."

Annie never answered about the dancing. She watched him wonder if she even spoke English. She infuriated men this way, turning them into fools for missing the signs. The women just smiled and touched her shoulder. But the bar back was cussing himself for making her feel uncomfortable.

"You fucking arsehole," he said.

He became a DJ and pretended to scratch records backward. When he started dancing, his arms straight along his legs, she didn't believe it for a long second. He kept on. She closed her teeth to keep from laughing, but he saw her smile. He got close and showed his watch, pointing to the time. He then revolved his finger until ten o'clock before dancing a long second.

"We'll go then," he said. "After work."

He talked like he'd spent a minute deciding that she could understand some words, but not every one. He went back to wiping down the clean bar. Annie might go and talk to him in a corner, but she wouldn't dance. She'd want to know if he understood women because of the way some men looked at him. She then watched Ron come slow from the men's room door. Whenever his hair was combed wet, she knew, he'd smell like nicotine and Vitalis. He passed the elevators, then looked at Jack filling pretzel bowls. He shook his finger.

"I'll catch you next time," he said.

Ron made Jack's eyes go dark. Annie could not imagine him

dancing in a club where men might look at him. His eyes, right then, didn't work with the spinning lights. They'd refuse the music like they'd ignore a river. But she pictured him talking on sidewalks, hating the concierge and pointing with a cigarette between his fingers. He'd vent for both of them, and she'd listen on the way to the train. He would be good for that.

After supper breaks, Annie and Ron waited for Jack to use the men's room, but he stayed behind the bar. He'd drunk three cappuccinos since dinner, and they knew he had to go, but he was cleaning the tap spouts to take his mind off it. He used Windex on the ashtrays.

"It's not long," Ron said to Annie. "He can't last."

Annie watched a new bellhop try bringing a luggage cart through the revolving door.

"You know," Ron said. "That bartender's got ten minutes."

The concierge took Annie's spot behind the desk because it was three steps nearer the men's room. He tapped his black Doc Martens. I've got shoe trees more expensive than these shoes, he'd say, but these are comfortable. They waited twenty more minutes for the bartender to break—when Jack walked off, he went fast and didn't move his arms. Ron was ten seconds behind him, and Annie saw the pocket-sized Vitalis in the breast of his Hilton blazer. She knew the time exactly from the big clock above the reception desk. It was ten minutes to ten.

The cop never asked Annie to stay, but he slept through the morning and breathed against her stomach.

She stroked his neck, using her knuckles, not her nails, and looked out his bedroom door. His apartment was white and without decoration. The floors were shiny and bare. She wondered if this sleeping cop thought himself a pedigreed dog kept in a private kennel. His space was for sleeping, eating, and pacing.

Annie looked at the cop's cheek and stroked her knuckles close to his throat. His breath was warm against her stomach before turning cold like the room. He'll like her orders, she thought, the subtle ones he doesn't know he is following, and after a time, he'll feel lost without them.

They lay together through the gray afternoon and the darkness that came very early. Annie loved his hand upon her hip, and the way he emptied his mind by breathing on her stomach. The cop was forgetting himself by using her scent. His wife was gone, his dream-thoughts random and even fleeting. She stroked his hair and watched him breathe doglike through his nose.

She might turn him into her jester, or the keeper of her cats, and he'd never know she had transformed him. Annie offered oblivion, and the cop had a loud silence. By tomorrow night, he'll understand he needed her scent to clear his head and imagine a future. Now, he saw everything through his wife's death, and his silence was frustration over not being able to outrun this dead woman. Without her, the cop will become junkie sick.

18

The wet snow fell two days before New Year's and melted before it hit the ground. The couples in matching fleeces walked among lit shop windows, still optimistic about one more holiday wine night with the few couples who'd stopped being as much fun. Mike turned the paddy wagon off Armitage, away from the white lights wound in the old trees, and mumbled the couples' names to himself—Michelle and David, Lisa and Patrick, Noah and Sarai. They'd all bought loft condos for the fast turnover, he thought, but none were flipping, even with the low mortgage rates, and the women had already started doing Google searches about fertility treatments. They were having big fantasies about space and privacy fences, now that proximity to shoe boutiques and bistro sea bass wasn't important. Mike imagined them telling their husbands that the property taxes weren't worth the city schools. The women wouldn't be able to let it go.

Today, he started the afternoon shift for a week, the four to midnight, where come eight PM the late-working investment bankers raced their Land Rovers down side streets. The cops called it the

Viagra 5K because anytime they made reckless driving stops, they found the individually wrapped blue pills in their pockets. Some of these guys aren't even thirty-five, Sergeant Olszewski said. It's a shame worse than letting your buddy jump your sister.

After eight, the night became a great movement of eighty-thousand-dollar vehicles the men bought to drive between the parking structures downtown and the garages included in the price of their condos. Overpriced metal, living rooms on wheels, the feeling of command. They took their moving violations like movie tickets, treating Mike with the same sarcastic politeness they used on the West Africans who valeted their cars. But there would never be a partner-of-the-day on afternoons. If the calls were slack, Mike could get away without smelling anybody for a straight four hours. When he turned on Lincoln, the streetlight was dry like the pavement.

He drove the wagon and looked at the black trees. Annie had needed the illusion of stealth to leave his apartment, and he didn't understand why. She'd known he was awake—her ear had been trained on his breath as if trying to translate a code—but she'd taken her chest off his back by degrees. He looked away, but his eyes never closed. She dressed in her wet silk without standing up. He then heard her bare feet on the oak floor. When she was gone, he felt the change immediately and Susan returned upon two legs.

Annie might tell him a sad story about herself, but she'd never let him use it to know her. Take her only when she comes, he reminded himself.

Mike went two blocks, past sports bar guys spilled onto sidewalks with crooked cigarettes, a Starbucks going into an old hot dog stand, then hit his blue lights so he could make a U-turn and head back northwest. In the end, he thought, a cop drove and looked around a lot. For him, the color of night was never different.

He suddenly stopped the wagon in traffic and put on the blue lights. The Audis and the BMWs passed him like basketball players who threw elbows when the referee turned away.

The man came running bearded and bald from the alley. He was naked and his legs were all white. He had a picture duct-taped to his chest, a large black and white print. When he ran across the sidewalk, his skin a blur in the light from the shop windows, he dangled his arms as if he'd been told to keep them a certain way. Mike thought he was going to run straight into the traffic and die naked. He'd expire with his arms spread affectedly, killed by the grill of a Lexus R620 with cattle guards and floodlights. But the guy stopped inside the line of parked cars, and checked to see if his arms were hanging the right way. Mike would have bet he was going toward the street.

He radioed and got out, then walked along the rowed cars. The guy stood checking his arms. He ran in place. His top teeth hit his lower ones. He kept dangling his arms.

"Go easy," Mike said. "You can slow it down to a stand."

"I got to run the road," he said. "My arms like this. I was told." Mike figured he'd been reduced to this in less than a minute.

"Who told you?" he said.

"American planes didn't napalm this village in the picture. He told me that. He said, 'We can't have this girl anymore.'"

"The village?" Mike said.

"In the picture."

The print taped to his chest was Kim Luc Phu running from the napalm and the humid wind that spread the flames from the village to the paddy docks. Her arms held a perfect seven and five o'clock, and so did the man's. The print was laminated enough to turn the rain. From memory, Mike knew the Vietnamese girl was naked, but he couldn't tell in the darkness. Suddenly he smelled Annie's rain scent and wondered if she ever ran from a burning village.

"We used these pictures wrongly," the guy said. "I know that now. We pissed all over what our brothers had died for."

"Go slower."

"I've got miles left to run. He told me to make like Paul Revere and tell the city what I know."

The guy had spat while he talked. His lips were blue. Mike watched his eyes and never saw him blink, then ripped the picture from his chest.

"Who taped this picture?"

"There are men watching. He told me I must run until everybody knows what he told me."

The man took off and ran headlong into traffic, past the twirling wagon lights, the tree shadows left by the streetlamps. He got hit fast: a restored Jeep Wagoneer with the original wood took him out at the knees, and he flew left, landing on an Audi hood. The guy had gone up with his arms down. The Jeep had stopped, the driver still a dark shape, but the traffic kept moving. Mike waved for the cars to slow, then stared past their headlights, trying to see if the guy was a mess. When he started into the street, he watched the man lying on the car hood, and tried to remember if Grant Hospital was closer than Illinois Masonic.

He walked and pushed the picture down into his pocket, feeling it wrinkle, and swore Dilger was lying about the Jiffy Lubes. He was on Lexapro or something. This killer was saying that humiliation never goes away, and if he will trouble himself to prove it with the old pictures that turned people against his war, it would be nothing for Dilger to lie about the Jiffy Lubes.

Mike took a breath before approaching the man, as if to keep Annie's rain smell in his nose.

19

The agency never called back about Annie. Four days now. Goetzler couldn't get Nick on the phone.

He sat in his Grand Cherokee, parked between twin Explorers, watching the cop buy a chicken sandwich from the Greek's. The *Tribune* was folded on the seat beside him, and he put his finger on the guy's picture in the Metro section: Mike Spence, dark-eyed in a police hat, his mouth tight like a closed tobacco pouch.

Goetzler knew this was the cop who beat the yuppie; he remembered the eyeballs that didn't move when he threw punches. That night, in the headlights, this cop had hit a man because he used hair gel the rain couldn't melt, and Goetzler loved him for it. He'd swung hard, as if he was fighting to remain himself and stay in uniform. *Honor and pride gets you detailed on the paddy wagon every time.*

He'd read about the cop saving Will Avers's life while he ate two scones and pushed the crumbs into the newspaper seam. The cop used a tourniquet above Avers's knee and saved his leg. He performed CPR on a car hood, beating Avers back to life with a fist against his heart. He took him to Grant Hospital himself, and again administered CPR outside the emergency room. Goetzler left the bookstore and drove Lincoln Park looking for the cop's wagon in the headlit dark—the article said he was the paddy driver, though never explained how he'd messed up to draw the detail. But he found the cop in three hours, double-parking in front of the Athenian Room (chicken on pita with fries: six bucks). From his picture, he thought the guy was a good shot, but a bad listener, the kind of man who only needed his own ideas.

Ecco Homo, Goetzler thought. Here is the man.

He bet the cop hadn't slipped on the sidewalk carrying Avers. It snowed that afternoon, then warmed, so the pavement was half sleet. He hoped Avers kept his hands spread like he'd been told, and his likeness to the girl in the picture made the cop laugh. The old hippie had a slouch from sleeping afternoons while hiding thirteen years from the FBI, and he ran in the way of people who don't run.

Goetzler had hid in Avers's garage for five hours, wearing a Henry Kissinger mask, the eyes cut larger for his glasses. He pulled the .38 while Avers stepped from his green Passat with two Whole Foods bags full of shiitake mushrooms and lemongrass. When Avers saw the pistol, his eyes went like wind, and he did what he was told: strip down and stand there. Goetzler taped the picture to his chest, using duct tape against the gray hair. Avers let him do his work. Goetzler then pointed to the girl in the picture, her open mouth, her tight face, and said, "None of us liked doing these things. They'd always send away the guys who did."

Avers kept quiet and lifted his foot off the cold cement.

"You need to know that. Men are there and things always go the wrong way. In Vietnam, nobody ever meant to do anything."

The man wasn't talking.

"Look down at the picture," Goetzler said.

Avers's eyes were like wiggling fingers. He'd been scared thoughtless.

"Your movement used this girl to make the world hate us, and we had no choice but to be in Vietnam. We were not lucky enough to stay behind."

Goetzler pointed the gun at the girl in the picture while Avers panted with calmed eyes.

"Do you understand your crime?"

Avers nodded. Goetzler knew the man could not speak.

"There are men with me," Goetzler lied. "They will have rifles trained on the route you must run while you mimic this picture. There are many of us who seek revenge, and we will always watch you. If you don't mime the little girl exactly, you'll also be shot."

When Goetzler opened the garage door, Avers started his route by sprinting, his arms dangling while his bare feet slapped the alley. This was a good night.

In the old days, he knew Uncle Kerm would comb his hair at the Drake and laugh big laughs over this gag. He'd want to hear the story a few times. No shit, he'd say. You made him run bare-ass naked.

Goetzler could never meet the cop, but he wondered what the picture of the running girl meant to him. This cop, he knew, hated the men he protected, and seeing Avers probably made him laugh. Goetzler imagined him keeping the picture and showing it to his cop buddies over Harp pints at Simpson's on Western Avenue. The guys would all want to buy Goetzler double Jamesons and shake his hand for giving them something to laugh about.

Later, when the cop left the Greek's, walking slow for the paddy wagon, Goetzler sat up, then cut NPR's local pledge drive off the radio. The cop held the sandwich in a white bag and stopped by the wagon door. He was tall and Spartan lean, and stared over the hood at the street. Goetzler rolled down the window, looking with the cop to see. The asphalt was wet enough to show the brake lights, and the alley went black and white for a mile.

20

Annie's last date was an Arab electronics salesman who wore Brut 33 and talked about doing big business in the new Iraq. CD burners, iPods, Discmans. Inside two years, he told Annie, every Iraqi would have something Sony in their ears. Hip-hop will be big, he said. When you break it down, Baghdad is no different than the Bronx. He lingered inside the doorway, asking for her cell number with swimming eyes.

"Mr. Di Franzo doesn't like us to do that," she said.

The Arab, like most men aware of Joey Di Franzo and his mad-rabbit face made famous by the *Sun-Times*, always disappeared when understanding Annie's agency kicked up to an Outfit guy. For the suburban johns, *The Sopranos* filled in their lapsed street experience, and mentioning an Italian name was enough to create colon spasms.

She didn't know if Nick kicked up to anybody, but Joey Di Franzo was the only Chicago mob name she'd heard. She paged through many newspapers doing day in-calls, and the reporters were forever claiming he ran the Outfit.

After the Arab left, Annie showered with Ivory soap and hot

hotel water for fifteen minutes before the Arab's cologne washed off. She sat on the Holiday Inn bed, drying herself, officially between clients. On the chair the guy's *Tribune* reeked of Brut 33, but the Metro section insert lay on top, and she saw the cop's picture.

The towel fell away from her breasts when she reached for the paper. Annie fanned the cologne off the newsprint while reading about the cop saving a john's life by taking him to Grant Hospital in the front seat of his paddy wagon. The cop even gave the john CPR at the last red light before the emergency room cul-de-sac.

Annie let her eyes bounce over the two words of his name like she was glancing at the license plate number on a parked car.

In the photo, the cop was again the runner from the window, not the sad man who needed her smell to sleep. Tonight, she decided he'd come to her because they were not together last night, and she'd watched him leave and return from a second run. She saw his TV light in the glass until dawn. The cop was a man who could only sedate his anger by exhaustion. But lying together, he was a thoughtless person, a man sleeping between her shows.

She dressed and walked out of the hotel room, ditching her next appointment. She was done washing their Walgreen's cologne off her breasts and stomach. She'd create an exclusive arrangement with Goetzler, though delay clarifying for him his confusion about Vietnam, and keep the sleepy cop for sex. If needed, she could always find another Nick.

The cop dripped in Annie's doorway, his leather jacket soaked to a glow, and the water spots dried black on the oak floor. His pistol was snapped into a holster and his radio drowned low. He looked like the cop in the *Tribune* picture, his cheekbones more definite, his lips thin. Annie suddenly felt cold. He didn't care about forgetting with her stomach.

Off the street, his eyes were still coplike, that look gotten from having let other men freeze his dreams about true love, and the more Annie searched them for softness, looking for a crack between the eye corner and the ball, she only noticed how his shirt pockets bore the ruin of a starch crease. She knew he liked starting his afternoon shift without wrinkles, hoping vaguely that he might move through the hours as a full participant without breaking starch.

Neither of us can admit we are of this world, she thought.

After the cop closed the door, the hall light disappeared from his wet leather jacket.

Annie turned off her cell and Nick's calling number left the screen. The cop was looking for a light switch, wall by wall, his eyes drawn like he was aiming. When he found it, the night turned on, and he took two pictures from his coat, holding up the prints left and right. Nguyen Ngoc Loan shooting the Viet Cong. Kim Luc Phu escaping fire from the sky. For the first time, she felt him disgusted over her being a hooker. He had the look of a transformed john who'd pay for the hour to try talking her from the life.

"You know these?" he said.

"I have four memories of Vietnam," Annie said. "Neither of those pictures are among them."

"This lawyer, Mike Rosen, was just murdered," he said. "The killer dressed him up like the VC. Then I saw a naked guy running an alley with this picture taped to his chest. Both of them were actively against the Vietnam War. The detectives won't do the work."

You did this for me, Goetzler? Annie thought. I bet you wish you could believe that.

"You looking for police rank?" she asked the cop. "Are you a lifer?"

"The killer's anger is toxic because many men will love him," he said. "I know his hate."

Annie smiled at the cop but her smile was lost upon him. She walked closer until he lowered the pictures. This cop, she decided, responded only to the questions he wished he were asked.

"These pictures started appearing after I met you," the cop said. "It must stop. I can't think about this killer's anger anymore."

"I allow you to sleep," she said. "That is all."

"Why did you start calling me soldier the first night?"

"Because you run like the soldiers on recruiting commercials."

"I want you to be more specific."

Annie smiled at his cop talk, the poetry of declarative sentences. Maybe he would go quiet and become the runner again.

"Only my face is Vietnamese," she finally said to him.

"You came to me in a white silk dress. I read that schoolgirls only wear the white *ao dai*. I think you are acting something out. You understand something about this killer."

Annie smiled and walked closer to Mike, but he was stiff like a room key. She let down her hair by pulling one pin. He didn't put away the pictures.

"Why did you keep calling me soldier?" he said again.

"An American Vietnamese would never do this. We can make too much money here. Why should we care about our bad memories?"

The cop moved the pictures closer to her by locking his elbows. Annie couldn't exhale easily, and she inched the air through her nose. From the paper weight, she knew the cop cut the prints from the same photographic history of the Vietnam War that Goetzler

kept on an end table. If Goetzler did this, Annie knew he took am-
phetamines to prolong his will; men like Donald Goetzler didn't
have very good legs, and displays of courage were artificially fueled.
She then pointed to Kim Luc Phu in the print and wondered, like
always, what she was screaming.

"This picture means something to me," she said.

The cop dropped his hands and let his eyes soften.

"Yes," she said. "Every night I thank God I wasn't that girl.
Who would want to be known forever as a nightmare?"

"Is that why you don't like being Vietnamese?"

"No," she said. "I just decided not to be a bad memory."

When she went to touch him, he recoiled, then stopped himself.
Her hands slid beneath his leather jacket and the leather made his
shirt warm enough for the starch to gum her palms. His ribs felt like
tool handles. She looked at his wet chin and he stared at the wall.

"I'll only do this once," she said.

She then raised her nails along his back, but he still didn't
move.

"You know something about this?"

"Yes," she said, "that you think too much about getting double
yolks in one egg."

He pushed away from her and turned on a heel, starting down
the stairs without closing her door. Annie thought she heard dogs.
She stood watching the cop, the way his shoulders receded to the
darkness, and disciplined herself not to think beyond her own
opinions.

Twenty minutes into a two-hour call, Annie sat on the couch,
Goetzler in the chair. He turned the brandy snifter in his hand,

making full circles, and looked at himself in the window. He'd lit a Cubano and let it burn and talked to her about flow theory, using a pen and a legal pad to demonstrate, but instead of looking at her, he followed the smoke up from the ashtray. Now, he was quiet and rocking the snifter without watching himself. Annie noticed the smoke slow before the cigar went out. She pointed to the ashtray.

"You do that because you can afford it?" she said.

He kept watching himself, his eyes like sky in wet windows. He'd started making small waves with the brandy. She waited, but he never asked her about the missed week.

"I like the smell of good cigars," Goetzler said, "not the smoke in my lungs." He hadn't wanted to talk.

Annie glanced again at the coffee tables, this time with one eye. Art books, Degas, Pissarro, Cezanne. Matthew Brady's Civil War pictures. But the photographic history of the Vietnam War was gone. She looked another time, her eyes wet from the old smoke. The book wasn't beneath the long lamp that he never lit.

"You should use that lamp," she said. It was copper and green-shaded, a library light.

Goetzler didn't look at her. He sank into the chair, one palm on the leather.

"It hits my eyes sideways," he said.

"Then move it."

"I bought the lamp for that table and this is my chair."

"It's a waste," she said.

They sat and looked together, trying to see the lake in the darkness. When Annie knew the book was gone, she uncrossed her legs and let herself become comfortable. In the glass, she watched herself smile before watching Goetzler set down the brandy. Tonight, he couldn't keep the act going: he quit the physics lesson too soon, and never told a war story. Annie then took off her boots and brought up her legs, marveling at what they'll do for a dream of themselves. For gratitude, she'd forget the envelope if Goetzler kept quiet and didn't touch her. But if he started with the stories, the offer didn't stand.

21

Mike went down into an alley puddle after the shadowed man hit him. He landed hard on his knees, and his heart punched from having just run six miles. Mike saw the legs of the others in the headlights before the man patted his face and pushed him back flat. He watched their ankles while they laughed like kenneled dogs. When the white flashlight hit his eyes, he felt his running shoes being taken off, then heard them hit the open Escalade doors. He thought himself the dived fighter in a boxing movie.

"The gook isn't your butterfly, copper," the man said. "The gook is someone's investment. Meaning, you don't let her fuck you for free. Do I need to keep talking?"

Mike listened for the other men, but they were quiet. He could not see their pants and shoes, only their ankles and shod feet.

"Just shake your fucking head and I'll go away forever."

Mike looked into the white light, hoping it would still his eyes.

"Fucking difficult prick," the man said.

Mike heard a click, then a flame pinched his wet-stockinged foot.

"This is just the Zippo," the man said. "Next time, I'm pouring on the fucking gas."

There were footsteps and closing doors before the headlights receded backward and the alley went dark. He lay alone, hemmed by streetlight, and believed every word they said. These men hoped they could avoid blood, too. Like cops, they were lifers at heart.

Annie was dead to him. It wasn't even a decision. Like most things in his life, she was a fantasy taken too far.

Come spring, Mike would leave these sad men for Mexico when the airfares dropped. Selling the condo would give him sixty grand after taxes. He'd forget the skyline, the pictures, and his reasons for writing the novel when he first took the 727 seat. He'd fly to Zihuatanejo in late May to see the mangoes and fresh-caught snappers hauled in cyclos, the wet-lipped women built like flour sacks and drinking Coke, then rent an Audi A-4 and drive the seaside road to Guatemala where the brown Pacific waves hit rocks and sprayed the asphalt. He'd use the windshield wipers and pretend it was an autumnal storm blown across Lake Michigan so the wave force wouldn't scare him. He knew this water got violent enough to slam a Ford Festiva against the kopje rock faces lining the shore, and he'd spend the extra money for the Audi.

But now, beaten in the puddle, he wasn't sure if he could leave and breathe easy and understand that most of your points were never truly made. This killer might follow him down to the sunshine. When Mike returned to Mexico with pencils, steno pads, and a lone sharpener, he didn't want to have any doubts about thinking he could incite any man to care about another's pain.

Mike and Susan went to Ixtapa in the off-season, $800 for air and eight nights at the Las Brisas, burnt-orange bungalows with *hammocks on the patios, but the water around the reefs was too muddy for snorkeling. In Chicago, he'd bought them fins, masks, and snorkels, not even considering the sea change of late June. He'd seen the price online and booked the trip. Susan had looked over his shoulder at the screen, and it didn't even bother him. In Mexico, he'd swim her into the schools of fish and they'd make love in the shallow water while the sailboats evaporated in the hard sunlight. Her wet hair would be dark like her eyes, and he'd taste the salt on her tongue. Most things between them, he believed, could get washed away. But the hot current hits Pacific Mexico from Tahiti, the concierge told him, and the water stays brown from May through the summer.*

They spent their days walking Zihuatanejo, near the muddy waterfront, the ocean roily and broken by waves. The gift shops were closed and nobody sold T-shirts near the wharf where fishermen muscled dying marlins from the paintless boats. Susan wore a white linen dress, the train above her ankles, and the wind blew the slack between her knees. All afternoon, she'd been calming him about the poor snorkeling conditions. He knew he was getting too mad, and the hotel had no responsibility to report the water visibility on its Web site, the way he'd told the concierge it did after calling him a "flimflam" man. But Mike couldn't forget the bilgey water, even if he understood his anger was about Todd not caring about his book, and the only stories he could tell were about how soldiers end up.

He pointed to the ruined bay, the reef hidden by the brown water. Susan smiled while dirty-legged children ran past, their tongues orange from papaya sorbet.

They practice the bait and switch here, he said.

You were never baited.

The water was blue on the Web site.

They push the season, Susan said. That's how they make money. The water is brown.

It's not the season, she said. That's why we got the price.

He looked at Susan in her white dress, then the palm shadows black on the yucca bushes. His wife was beautiful, her hips soft in the linen. When he found her eyes again, she blew air like it was cigarette smoke. He looked back at the palm shadows.

We don't need snorkeling, she said of his plan.

It would be better.

I wouldn't like the fish swimming up against me.

They're wet like the water, he said. You wouldn't even know.

I'd see them doing it, she said, and I'd convince myself I felt them.

You sure about that?

You know how I am.

When they rode back to Las Brisas and their bungalow air-conditioned enough to chill brewed coffee, the highway was closed by a toxic spill, anhydrous fertilizer running from a tipped truck, and the bus took a coastal road where the Pacific waves rose and broke on the craggy asphalt. The coach was empty except for the thin man playing a guitar in the open doorway: "La Bamba" on cat-gut strings, the musician's pant legs wet from the salt spray. Mike watched Susan hold the seat edge and bounce with the bus, her face red from sun and motion sickness, then closed his eyes against seeing the wrecked ocean, listening to the stranger sing.

In the precinct lot, Mike Spence stood on the milk crate, his coat open, and hosed down the wagon floor before starting his shift. The cigarette butts shot against the front wall, bounced, then flushed back over the rear bumper. When he'd frisk a wagon mope, the jukebox drinkers, the ex-cons happy they could have a pizza sent to the bar, he took their cigarettes, but some left on benders expecting the flex-cuffs and the wagon, so they hid cigarettes in their shoes. Mike never figured how they smoked Kools with bound hands; no mope ever looked limber enough to hold a squat. He thought about the possible contortions while he hosed, and decided they used their teeth and farmer matches. He sprayed the butts down the grated manhole cover.

When he touched the welt on his cheek, he saw his breath in the dark, and his gloved finger came away wet. He'd broken the scab again and the cold stung his warm, thin blood. For some reason, he kept checking to see if the welt was still there, even after he'd made himself quit.

He figured Annie was a hooker because she believed she needed the cash to leave a world within fifteen minutes. She'd never stopped being a boat person. At night, he watched her come and go in cars, always dressed beyond the neighborhood, black suits and boots. In the late morning, before his shift, he'd watch her skip rope through the windows, and then do handstands. But he felt she was a hooker by the way she kept running her fingers when he'd stood stiff and thought of old trees. Call girls touched with typist hands, but Annie floated you over the rocks and disappeared like a cut-loose kite.

When he stayed the hose gun to hear the water run into the sewer, Kenjuan Mills walked up in the light rain. He decided to stop understanding the killer's side.

"It's picture-in-the-paper," Mills was saying. "The hero on the shit wagon. The Phoenix."

Before Mike looked at Mills, he'd already imagined the oldest guy in a ghetto club. All week, the sergeant walked the precinct house in his hooded leather jacket, telling guys how wise he was for moving to the West Side and leasing a BMW 529I. All the trim needs to see is the car, he'd say. The K-Town Niggers don't bother it because my bull sleeps in the garage. Mike kept seeing Mills taking Lakeshore Drive, wearing sunglasses in the dark, and sipping a glass of Heidsieck Brut. He laughed about it for a morning.

"Picture-in-the-paper," Mills said again.

Mike was silent. The water slowed into the sewer.

"Fuck up and move up," Mills said. "You're a combat hero now."

"It didn't get me off the wagon."

"You'll stay on the wagon even after they offer you tac squad again," Mills said. "The paddy will take your edge."

Mills smiled his gold teeth and pulled the hood over his eyes.

Mike Spence eyed the wet wagon floor, watching Mills cut the end from a Cohiba. Now, the only water running down the sewer was the spray from the black cleaning hose. Mike looked at the sergeant's gold teeth while he flashed his gold Rolex. He got his picture in the paper, and the captain never called him into the office. Mike could set the bomb timer by tipping the *Tribune* reporter who put him on page one of the Metro section, he thought, then resign from the department by leaving his badge on a urinal mint.

After duty, Mike drank the squad room's machine instant, his boots wet from the hose. He'd squared his schedule with Olszewski. They were giving him floating days off, Tuesday and Thursday, Saturday and Wednesday, and he'd worked nine shifts without a break. He couldn't shake the feeling of the paddy's wheel in his hands, sticky from old donut glaze, and spent the day between his shifts washing them like a dentist. By contract, the cops got two days consecutive, and they couldn't float on you without overtime. The clause never worked for his schedule. He started thinking the inside was against him, the cops within the cops, like *Serpico,* but they had no reason. One night, Olszewski called him to apologize. Shit, Spence, he said, I have a hard time remembering you. You're in-the-walls to me. But Olszewski never fixed it.

He was waiting to spot Ruiz. The detective always took coffee before hitting the Indiana casinos, and he was then walking down the stairs at the end of the hall. Mike needed to know if Ruiz was a drama cop or plain stupid.

Mike blew the steam off the paper cup, wishing the department was burying the pictures for a reason. He imagined the guys pulling their ties loose and rocking back on their heels. They'd made their side pure by treating the prints like Chinese menus dropped in doorways. They'd know they did. This killer is our brother, they'd say. How can we send him to the Sodomites. But Mike figured Ruiz wouldn't know what the pictures meant. Just some sick bullshit, he'd say. Ruiz was a clerk for the dead who subscribed to MILF porn sites, and with Avers in Belize on academic leave, refusing comment, he had no reason to remember the prints.

In the squad room, Ruiz's leather collar, wet from neck sweat, held the light. He poked the coffee machine button with a gloved finger, hazelnut and cream. Lately, depending on his jacket, he'd started wearing gray or black leather gloves. I got the idea, he'd brag, reading *Latin GQ* on the can.

Mike listened to the coffee spout.

"How's every little thing hanging," Ruiz said.

He hadn't turned from the machine. He smelled like White Castles.

"You know how I saw you look at me?" he said. "You noticed I wasn't watching."

"I don't know."

"I can see sideways," he said.

Ruiz still wasn't looking at Mike. He nodded while his coffee brewed.

"This homeboy," he said, "can watch booty pop on both sides of the street."

"Sure," Mike said.

Ruiz took a cup before getting the sugar cubes from his pocket.

"You even realize what some shit that is?" he said.

"You got something with it," Mike said.

Ruiz took red licorice from his pocket. He smiled and chewed, one hand candy, the other coffee. When he finished, he laughed to himself, holding up the cup and a finger. You got a mommie, here, he said. Then another mommie there. I have threesome fantasies running all day. Ruiz nodded, kissing the air. He then pulled the licorice too hard from his pocket. The strands, ribbed to a swirl, fell from the bag, and lay on the tiles like cut wire. He winked at Mike, turning up his hands, then walked from the room. Mike picked up the licorice and understood Ruiz hadn't even known what the picture meant. If Mike wanted, he could take this one right away from them. The pictures only stood for time away from Ruiz's threesome fantasies.

22

Today, Goetzler let Annie buy him lunch. She hadn't lined her eyes with mascara, and her lips were dry. Last appointment, she'd left the envelope on the foyer table, and lipsticked her cell number on the bathroom mirror, showing she got the joke by using quotation marks. He called her and asked her to lunch. I will pay, she'd told him before picking the place: New Saigon on Argyle, a storefront off the curb where Tuan's wife cooked in the steam from large pots, and the smoking Vietnamese drank iced coffee white from condensed milk. Now, Goetzler couldn't relax with Annie always looking at him. He'd dreamed this lunch for three days, imagining Annie taking his hand while the snow fell between the branches in Lincoln Park, and later, making love to him for nothing. *All I did was remind a few people of what happened in Vietnam, he'd tell her. How can they keep making judgments when they never saw blood?* Now, he couldn't keep his throat wet.

"You look different in a different place," she said.

He studied his reflection in the window to see. He was subtle and looked sideways at himself.

"I doubt you could notice it," she said. "It's just a way you are in the world. Like the difference between a man in a suit and a man in his stained lounging sweats."

Before he answered, Tuan brought the *pho* steaming in white porcelain bowls. He came bird-legged, like a hopping egret, Goetzler thought, his stocking feet small in his sandals. He set the noodle soup down, then the plate of limes, bean sprouts, and basil sprigs, trying to save face and not look at Annie first. After Goetzler had ordered, Tuan did his routine about working for the CIA and doing a hard nine in a reeducation camp far north of Hanoi.

"I started fighting the VC at seventeen," he said again. "I was a Special Forces interpreter in Can Tho. I work for Americans until 1975. The communists had my name on a list with a picture."

Goetzler pretended Annie was gone, then exhaled.

"They must have wanted you."

"They came looking for me. They interrogated my mother for three days."

"You must have been well connected," Goetzler said.

"My father worked for the French. They kept me in leg chains for one year."

Tuan was very proud and he turned on a heel. His wife kept a small Buddhist shrine by the cash register, and she'd left two Dunkin' Donuts glazed for her dead relatives.

Annie opened her eyes wide, then smiled, before laughing at herself, and tarring the basil leaves three times. She wanted all of her actions inside quotation marks. She piled the green pieces in her palm, then sprinkled the flecks into the *pho* broth, the steam a quarter gone. Goetzler looked away first. He listened to her clean her palms with a napkin she'd dunked into her water glass.

"You don't use the herbs?" she said.

"No."

"You should squeeze in lime. Put in bean sprouts, jalapeño pepper."

He knew Annie wasn't thinking what she spoke.

"It clouds the broth," he said.

"You've never had *pho* in Vietnam."

"Then," he said, "I liked it clear, too."

Annie smiled and drank the broth from the spoon. She then scanned the place.

"You did it for this?"

Goetzler pretended she didn't ask a question. She couldn't know unless he'd told her.

Tuan brought *pho* for the woman at the next table. Her cheeks were lighter than her face, and she held the noodles between her chopsticks, looking at Goetzler. She didn't act like the steam burned her knuckles. Tuan was watching Annie remake her ponytail without removing the band. The woman said to Goetzler, "I am Cambodian. Not Vietnamese."

"Not the same thing," Tuan said. "Your girl here knows that, Donald Goetzler."

He'd noticed the woman liked clear broth. Beside him, Annie sat in an odd nimbus of calm. He figured she'd float away until the people stopped talking.

Tuan was nodding like he'd won something by having remembered Goetzler's first name.

"Cambodians steal all the time," he said.

The woman, her eyes black, stared at Goetzler and nodded.

"They steal your sandals when you go walking," she said.

"They kill you first." Tuan was laughing.

"I never got killed."

"They shot Vietnamese soldiers for their sandals," Tuan said.

"The Khmer Rouge took mine when I carried my six-year-old brother to Thailand. They just ordered them off. I'd hear them in distant villages, the gunfire sounding like a waterfall, but they were never in my way again. My brother is a schoolteacher now. He's taking classes to be a principal."

"I escaped Vietnam on a boat," Tuan said. "Three tries. Once from Nha Trang, Vung Tau, then I went to Can Tho and came out the Mekong River. There were sharks in the ocean. They swam very close to the boat."

"I spent six years in a refugee camp."

"I was in Indonesia for two years after communist prison."

The woman smiled at Goetzler and let the noodles slide off her chopsticks. Her thumb and forefinger were red from squeezing. They started speaking Vietnamese, and Tuan sounded like a mad cat. He put his finger in her face, but the woman's eyes remained wide.

Goetzler turned to Annie. Her lips were flat. She made her finger a pistol and held it against an imaginary person's temple. Goetzler watched her laugh her mouth open, then fall silent, before drawing a smile on her face. When she pointed at him, like Tuan did the woman, Goetzler didn't know what to do with his hands.

23

Annie's neck and lower back felt slack. Her limberness from morning yoga had lasted past noon. She sat on the restaurant chair and lifted both legs, assuming the lotus, her legs crossed, her stocking toes tucked beneath her knees. She then watched Goetzler look away, out into the cold sunlight and its glints on the gutter ice, and drink his water wedged with lime. His eyes didn't blink. She wondered when he'd realized why they were meeting in public, then said, "Was the Viet Cong dead in the picture? He could have been dead and not known it yet. Maybe he died in the next frame?"

Goetzler nodded. Tuan wiped tables. Their reflections were stamped in the window glass like that.

"You may have reached a better understanding by now," she said.

He was quiet.

"You probably did the equation which determined it."

"The Viet Cong was dead," he said.

"You can say that now?"

"I could say it then."

"Either way," she said. "You and I will work out an arrangement."

Goetzler drank the water and his lips stayed wet. He refilled the glass, widening his eyes to keep from blinking.

"We'll set a donation schedule," Annie said.

He was looking at his hands. He drank again like he'd forgotten his last sip.

"But you and I will be exclusive lunch dates."

She wrote five thousand on a napkin and pushed it through a *pho* spill on the table. The numbers blurred but remained visible. He pushed back in his chair and sat with his legs stretched, staring between his shoes, his shoulders wilting, his stomach pooched, a water line running down his chin. Tuan walked smiling back to the kitchen.

"Every week," she said.

"How long?"

"I will be like your wife."

"I can do this for three years."

"Then I will divorce you."

"I understand."

"What do you understand?" she said.

"Nothing," Goetzler said. "But I had reasons."

"Revenge against the people who laughed at you when they were right."

"No," he said.

Annie kept quiet and smiled without showing teeth. She could get the money from Goetzler and give him to the cop. They could work out a deal that way. But the cop must know that the pictures were hers to use, not his. He was a voyeur like his country and he must understand that before he could use her stomach to sleep without the dreams. She had first call with the pictures and Goetzler would pay for the cop to understand that.

24

Mike Spence waited for the reporter at the Starbucks on Lincoln and Barry where the tattooed baristas wore combat boots and bomber jackets from the Army-Navy store up the street. He sat in a window seat while a girl with inch holes in her earlobes filled the pastry case with pumpkin bars. He didn't think much of the reporter, a thirty-something sleeper who believed himself Jimmy Breslin, but the pictures were bigger than Mike giving Avers CPR at a red light.

Mike would use a pay phone the day he called to resign from the department. Olszewski might ask him who he was, and Mike would tell the sergeant he was having a bonded Pinkerton deliver his H&K Nine. I left the badge on a urinal mint, he'd tell him. Now guess which men's room? Olszewski's problem was that he'd become immune to caffeine and nothing stirred him anymore.

Mike sipped his mint tea and touched his cheek as if reminding himself to forget the woman. He was feeling the hardened scab when Cam Samson, the reporter, walked in from the cold. Samson looked at Mike and brushed the lint from his cashmere topcoat.

"What do you got for me?" he said.

Samson sat on the chair beside him. He didn't take off his coat or gloves. Mike thought him the short guy who wore a different suit a day, Armanis and Polos from Filene's Basement, and taught a journalism class at City Colleges to pay the dry-cleaning bill. Mike then took the crumpled picture of Kim Luc Phu running from her napalmed village and laid it on the table.

"Remember the guy I saved?" Mike said.

Samson feigned having to recall by tapping a pen on the table. He wore a gold Seiko that looked like an oyster Rolex, but had only two pairs of Cole Haan shoes, brown and black, that he alternated daily. He tapped harder when he let himself notice the picture.

"That ex-Rainman?" Samson said.

Mike wished he'd quit with the pen.

"Will Avers," Mike said. "He had this picture taped to his chest."

"How come you have it?"

"I tore it off his chest before he ran into the street and got hit. He was told to mimic the little girl."

Samson held up his hand and looked away from the picture.

"You tampered with evidence," Samson said. "They will eat you if I write this up. But honestly, I don't want the cops mad at me. A Metro reporter needs the cops, so I'm not touching this."

"There's more."

Samson's cell phone went off in his pocket. He took the call and waved at Mike while he walked out the door. The wind lifted his coattails while he crossed Lincoln Avenue. Mike noticed he'd left his pen on the table. Samson was a sleeper and now the pictures were Mike's to remember or forget.

———

Argyle Street was Vietnam on Chicago blacktop. There were four blocks of boat people and their American children, *pho* shops made from old Irish taverns, jade stores selling Lincoln Park blondes green marble, and travel agencies run by former Saigon marines (Chicago to Ho Chi Minh City $969.69), all serviced by the dark-girdered El stop where roosting pigeons were unmoved by the trains.

Mike drove slow and close to the parked cars so the blue city trucks could pass him. The laminated pictures were taped to his dashboard, General Loan and Kim Luc Phu.

If Mike pursued the crime, he'd inherit what the man carried, and he didn't want to imagine his story anymore. Nobody wanted to remember old wounds, and Vietnam was America's worst memory. A blue stocking or a lawsuit will get this accidental killer, and Mike knew that thinking anymore about Vietnam would do him no good. But he still wanted to know if the killer was a round-eye from these alleys or the cornfields beyond the city.

Mike looked for connections between the prints and the Vietnamese on the sidewalks, the crew-cut gang boys lighting Kools in doorways, the women who still walked with paddy stoops, searching their eyes for the hysteria of those old moments. But among the barbecued ducks hooked behind windows, the thin people walked their shadows into the sidewalks, carrying gallon jugs of fish sauce. They remained unfazed by Malaysian pirates, Viet Cong extortionists, the guards at Filipino refugee camps, and were happy they could open restaurants and return to Vietnam with ten thousand dollars in twenties, even if the long flight to Ho Chi Minh City reminded them of standing upright in a boat. Annie was correct. In America, the Vietnamese sought repose, not revenge. He decided the man who killed Rosen and set Avers to running with flailing arms had always wished he could have done the same thing.

The killer was a fool who would catch himself. The lone difference between him and Rosen was military service in Southeast Asia, and the killer couldn't see that. His acting took slow years to prompt, and this revenge with old pictures was the revised work of many daydreamed scenarios. Mike also knew the killing of Rosen was an accident. This man wanted only to avenge humiliation. The first time with Rosen, he must have gotten stage fright and things went wrong.

Mike left Little Saigon by turning south on Broadway. The day was warming fast and smelled like rain. He tore the pictures from the dash without watching and threw them into traffic. Mike knew the killer was an American man, but after a childhood among the silos and stove factories of Watega, Illinois, he wanted nothing more to do with the anger those men taught him.

When he was a child in Watega County, he never heard the word Vietnam when it was said. It was spoken, like hello or turn left, but the constant repeating made the word seem soundless. He'd hear the word, then he wouldn't hear it.

Men in flannel shirts said Vietnam from bar stools, coffee counters, and diner booths. They spoke the word in the bleachers of high school football games, the Saturday line at hardware stores, hunting trips with their sons and nephews. After they'd told their happy drunk stories, the crazy girls in Melbourne, the boozy smell of the R&R plane, the word made them quietly angry, and many knew they couldn't begin to say what they felt. The smartest ones, the high school history teachers and the accountants, conjured conspiracy theories about Mao forcing Nixon to sell out the American soldiers if they were to be happy together. But the men like Mike's Uncle Jack, the welders and the carpenters, only plied their trade and went through a few wives. They bought wooded lots on Illinois rivers and kept captured North

Vietnamese army battle flags in their workshops, hanging them beside pictures of the Iwo Jima Memorial. After work, they drank in riverfront taverns and told their sad stories until the stories themselves became soundless like the word Vietnam.

As a boy, Mike watched the men who did not say the word, the high school English teachers and the divorce lawyers, create a society away from veterans like his uncle Jack. He also watched them silently measure themselves against the veterans, seek therapists who didn't care about controlling the answer, and learn to half believe their created ideas of themselves. But the word ruined them the way it did the veterans. Neither side could admit they'd allowed their fathers to make Vietnam a word. They remained guilty and furious about it, like Isaac refusing to see Abraham's knife.

Mike drove Western Avenue north for a ride and soon found himself among twenty used car lots. The prices were soaped into the windshields, or sometimes the financing terms, and the old cars were mostly sold by their new paint jobs. At the red light, south of Petersen, he stared at the cars and wished the green would come sooner.

That night, Mike sprinted down Claremont Street and his block was dark save for the shaded light behind the three-flat windows. The streetlights were out. He did not see the rain, but it sounded on the car hoods and bleared the blinking red alarm lights in the drivers' windows. He'd run Ravenswood to Petersen Avenue and back, along the tracks, never breathing easy, and sliding on the wet asphalt without falling down. His lungs stayed stiff and never sucked with his strides. But he'd made the seven miles, breathing through his nose, always ready to slip from the slick leaves.

In two days, Mike Spence would head for Mexico and the ocean on the Ixtapa-Las Brisas Web site. The water wasn't clear enough to show the bottom, but it was clean and blue. He'd sea-kayak after patio coffee, the sunlight yellow, the morning wind headlong and damp, and if the waves tipped him, he'd roll the kayak and continue wet. He knew nothing about paddling, save from books, but the roll would come quickly because he understood how to make them fail. Finesse, he read, beats raw strength when attempting to recover a kayak.

In Mexico, he thought, he could find Susan again and tell her that the cloudy water was his perception and nothing else. He might sleep a whole lot better.

That morning, he lay his badge on a urinal mint in the precinct house, then used a supermarket pay phone to resign from the department. He only told Olszewski that he was no lifer, then left the receiver dangling while a Latina checker looked at him without interest. He retained a real estate agent, a pregnant blonde, even if condos outstocked hubcaps in Chicago. You'll clear a hundred thousand, she claimed. There's no cash but the interest rates are low.

He ran through the alley puddles while the garage doors turned the rain. When he slowed into the walk-off, his legs remained strong, but inflexible, and he didn't feel his knees bend. The pain went from his hips to his ankles. He slapped his thighs. He squeezed them.

Mike was looking up when Annie stepped from between the garages. The lights from the used car lot bled on her vinyl raincoat.

"Your windows are dark," she said.

"Go," Mike said. He kept walking for the gangway.

"I didn't have you beaten. That happened."

"Random like my wife?" he said.

"I watch you hide," she said. "Every night."

He stopped and looked at the alley. Foamy water ran from gutter spouts and made the puddles eddy.

"Hiders know hiders," she said. "And we only admit we hide to people who don't. We never confess to each other."

He walked between the garages and she followed him. The rain tapped her coat while it cut through their shadows on the bricks. His footfalls squeezed the puddle water from his shoes. Her shadow then closed with his by taking three steps to his one.

"I know the man isn't Vietnamese," she said.

"You told me that," he said.

"It's not my guess now," she said. "He is a john."

"I know that about you," he said. Mike stopped before the steps. He'd talked without looking back.

"The killer's never had sex with me," she said, "but you have. He also pays."

"I was with you three times."

"Did you know my name?"

"I'm not a john."

"You all marry," she said, "then become johns. This killer is no different."

"I know a detective you can call. Manny Ruiz at the Twelfth."

"We'll get his money, then I'll give him to you."

"You can call the murder hotline and inform anytime."

Annie waded through the long puddle and he knew she was breaking the reflected house light. He could beat her up the stairs if he thought of running bleacher drills, but the door key was through his shoelace, and she'd catch him when he knelt to undo it.

"You both see my face," she said, "but not my eyes. That is how johns look at you."

"I'm not looking at you."

"You and she would silhouette yourselves in the window. I know how you see me."

Mike was silent.

"This man had ideas like that," she said.

"I'm done," he said.

The rain disappeared into his sweatshirt and bounced off her vinyl jacket. It tapped the puddle while she stirred the dark water with her boots. She wrapped her arms around his elbows, and he felt her face sideways against his wet back. She laughed, shrieks like fighting cats.

Mike watched her fingers touch beneath his chest before he strained his sore thighs and reared back. She stood laughing. He grabbed her wrists and pushed her hands off him, then bucked hard until he felt her fall away. He pulled off his running shoe and sprinted upstairs untying the key.

25

For lunch, Annie picked Wicker Park bistros, restaurants with changing names, and hardly touched her veal entrees. She demanded fifty-year-old port and took one sip, then cappuccino with Frangelico, which turned cold. She ordered paté and crème brûlée and flourless chocolate cake. When they'd leave, an hour exactly, her plates remained full, looking like a buffet, and Goetzler laughed to keep from crying because noontime with Annie now cost him twenty thousand dollars. Last week, she'd written the increase on a napkin, *Lunch = 20K*, then pushed it through the risotto crumbs, telling Goetzler to bring the envelopes taped in French *Vogue*. It has better perfume samples, she'd said. He could last a year like this, before going broke, the condo sold, the Jeep Cherokee classified in the *Sun-Times*, or move to a Northwest Side three-flat with hissing steam heaters, and have nothing in two years.

Tonight, Goetzler sat in the Athenian Room, nursing a chicken pita with fries. Danny Partikis grilled thirty chicken breasts, an order from the firehouse on Halsted, and the flames jumped while he basted them with lemon juice and butter. He was a smiley guy who never talked, so rich and silent that people thought him an idiot savant. Goetzler watched him work the paintbrush against the chicken, the grill fire hissing, then popped the Rolex from his leather cuff, deciding a pawn would get him three grand, but a straight sale might bring six. He'd already waited two hours for the cop, and it was ten-fifteen, forty-five minutes until another punishment took over the wagon. He'd started thinking about other things. Just because the cop would never let a hooker squeeze him, this man who wore his paddy detail like an Iron Cross, didn't mean Goetzler could watch him eat a gyro and absorb his will.

Partikis made the sandwiches, chicken and pita with lettuce and tomato, then rolled them in foil. He played Greek dance music, mandolins done techno, and bobbed his head while he dropped them into the white bags.

Goetzler brought his tray to the garbage can when Partikis started making French fries. He looked at his hairy wrists, flecked with tomato seeds, and saw no watch. Partikis didn't even own a Walgreen's Timex, but Goetzler smiled, knowing a rich Greek loves a deal. He took off his Rolex.

"I got something here," Goetzler said.

Partikis looked up from the deep fryer. The grease hit his arm but he did not move it.

"Since 9/11," he said, "I could have your Rolexes on both my wrists and ankles. Two of them."

Goetzler put the watch in his palm, arranging it as if displayed. He'd taken care.

"Four thousand," he said.

"You people won't quit with the watches," he said. "I could buy two Rolexes a week. Even Cartier."

"Thirty-five hundred."

"Why should I buy a watch when I can ask you the time?"

Goetzler listened to the grease. He'd even wondered if Partikis had first heard him over the noise.

"If you people spend big money on watches," Partikis said, "I figure you must not mind."

"I could pawn it for three grand."

"That's what I tell the other guys to do," he said.

Partikis emptied the baskets in the tray beneath the heat lamps. He returned to smiling about nothing and salted the French fries. Goetzler put the Rolex in his coat pocket like it was register change, then watched Partikis bury the sound of sizzling grease with the electronic music. The Greek started dancing while standing very still and bagging the fries. Goetzler left and didn't know it was raining until he got inside his Jeep Cherokee.

In 1982, Uncle Kerm bought a new Cadillac Seville two weeks before colon cancer killed Goetzler's father. He got it from a Melrose Park Italian he'd let do six months on a weapon's violation instead of facing second-degree murder charges. This was the last year of the hatched back ends, and Bobby Odo had a champagne color, the leather seats a shade lighter than the body paint. There were five hundred miles on the odometer, and the car smelled of cigar brands that Kerm didn't smoke.

But the Cadillac was new: the oil hadn't been changed, and the seat never molded to Odo's backside, thick from prison carbohydrates. First thing, Kerm drove to Daytona because he was retired, and took a redheaded schoolteacher just turned forty-one. Goetzler imagined him holding the wheel with one hand, smiling more about the new car than this younger woman who had a thing for hotel rooms. Full sticker is for stiffs, Donny, he'd say.

Before Goetzler's father died, he lay in the hospital sheets, whiter than the walls at Resurrection Hospital, asking Goetzler when Kerm was coming. Goetzler figured his uncle was shacked up and he just didn't know where. The old man was calling his little brother "the shot," shortened from big shot, never knowing he cuckolded him for ten years. Last year, Goetzler's mother died from Lou Gehrig's, and after her funeral at Rago's, Kerm walked his father to the parking lot, perhaps intending a confession. They only talked about selling the farm in Gray's Lake because they'd stopped hunting together.

"There's no aptitude test to be a cop," his father told Goetzler from the bed, "but you know there's one to be a machinist."

He'd learned not to hear him.

When Kerm returned with the grapefruit and the Clementine oranges, Goetzler's father was already displayed at Rago's. He came to the funeral parlor in a wrinkled madras, having seen the *Tribune*'s obituaries, and complaining about the traffic back from the schoolteacher's condo in Lincolnwood. I found a Chicago paper north of Indianapolis, he'd said. The broad saw our name. Goetzler stood in his Weber Industrial Supply suit, charcoal gray, waiting for Kerm to notice his new gold oyster Rolex, but his uncle only talked about steak houses in Cincinnati.

Goetzler's father had coworkers, guys like him who wore windbreakers to mass, but not friends. They left the wake after shaking his hand for the second time, and never gathered for Early Times and Schlitz. Afterward, Kerm ducked the priest and drove Goetzler down Lincoln Avenue in the rain, headed for the Fireside Inn on Wells Street because he knew the bartender poured heavy if you tipped a five after the first drink. There were still lipsticked Salem butts in the ashtray from the Florida trip, a half-full pint of peppermint schnapps under the passenger seat.

He held the wheel with two fingers and sank into the bench seat the way Goetzler imagined him doing on I-65. His brother was dead from colon cancer, but Kerm played Brubeck's "Blue Rondo a la Turk" on the eight-track and made smoke rings.

"Cincinnati had the best meat by far," he said.

"Howard Street," Goetzler said. "By the river."

"How'd you know?"

"Weber flew me down," he said. "I ran focus groups of electrical contractors. I'm studying the catalog's effectiveness on contractors in the Ohio River valley."

Uncle Kerm lit another Camel filter while he broke for the red light. The back tires locked and Goetzler felt them fishtail. He sat up in his seat.

"This schoolteacher," Kerm said. "She'd go hootchie for a T-bone and a motel room. Just dirty like some guys talk about."

Goetzler put his watch wrist on the armrest. He pushed back his jacket cuff.

"Is she a friend?"

"I know her." Kerm then looked at Goetzler, the stoplight sheening his cheek. "You know," he said.

"You meet her at the Drake?"

Kerm nodded and stared at the red light.

"You must have gotten her oysters?" Goetzler said. He lifted his wrist and the Rolex caught the dash light.

"It was this car," he said. "That's what got her to Florida."

"She wouldn't joy ride all the way to Daytona. Maybe to Oak Park."

"It was about the car when I was twenty-five," he said.

"Seventeen hours one way?" Goetzler feigned cool. "She liked you."

Kerm smiled and tapped his cigarette ash through the cracked window, then wiped dry the stray raindrops on his thigh. He hadn't yet looked at the Rolex. Goetzler bought the watch thinking his father's bungalow would sell by next month, and he figured Kerm knew it. You can only buy a Rolex with the cash you score, he'd tell him at the restaurant. The light remained red.

"The woman's waist was tight," Kerm said. "She'd do her Jane Fonda workout in the motel rooms."

"Tights and leg warmers?" Goetzler asked.

"The whole nine."

"She's looking for a father. She'd love you forever."

Kerm squinted his eyes and gauged Goetzler's seriousness.

"You don't got a prayer, Donny," he said. "You know that."

"You could be happy."

"I keep forgetting you came from your old man."

When the stoplight changed, Kerm's foot fell heavy on the accelerator, and the engine dragged the Cadillac down Lincoln. His uncle passed stuffed buses on the yellow line, the oncoming traffic honking and pulling close to the parked cars. The tires broke the light-bleary puddles and the speed forced Goetzler's scalp into the headrest. Kerm kept a straight face, his blue eyes hidden away, and blew smoke rings at the wet windshield while he jumped the red light at Halsted and Fullerton. Goetzler looked at the Rolex, realizing it had stopped during his father's visitation.

Goetzler drove around Annie's block for the seventh time, wishing he'd put the .38 in his coat pocket instead of between his pant waist and hip. The gunmetal pinched his skin when he turned a corner. A welt was forming, and it would turn raw after three more circles. But Goetzler decided he shouldn't move the pistol into his pocket with the silencer he'd made with a socket set from an Internet diagram. Changing his mind to avoid pain had become too much of a habit.

Goetzler would fire two bullets into Annie's ceiling, then put the pistol to her forehead, reminding the hooker that she was bluffing. Goetzler figured Annie was too selfish to split this money, and after three days of her pimp stonewalling him, he believed that he was about to cut her loose. But Annie could keep the money he'd given her. He owed her a chance at the straight life. He also knew the cop would understand all of this. The wagon driver could never know, but he'd silently nod if he ever heard about it.

He'd scare her silent. Maybe turn her into a wall-eyed cat.

The last pass, he'd noticed light in her two-flat window, a vague yellowing of the glass. He knew her radiator hissed steam even if the January cold never returned when the rains quit. By law, the boilers were on timers from November to April. The apartment would be humid and breathless, and she might have opened her back window so the lake air could cool the hardwood rooms. He'd go inside face first with his pistol extended, and keep his money. Now, she was the VC.

Stay squared away, Goetzler, and you'll own the glory road.

26

The mirror where Annie watched herself hold the yoga plank fogged and dripped. The open windows did nothing against the steamy registers, and the heat made vague clouds outside the screens.

The cop was Vietnam-gone to her. She imagined her hands would always go through him when they touched. She wanted a quiet mind and tonight she'd breathe until she met the stillness. The cop was her wish, not a real man.

Her stomach throbbed from the yoga positions, but she was happy to know the sequence, the dying warrior, the downward dog, the fawn, and didn't need a brick keeping the book opened flat. When the sweat started, wetting her black bra straps, she knew her gray tom would come from under the bed and lick the salty water from her obliques, slapping her face with his tail.

The plank numbed her waist while she waited for the cat. He was still hidden away, scared by the street noise. She breathed like slow rain, and decided she'd take Goetzler's money until she had one hundred thousand dollars. She'd split the sum between four banks, then cage her cats and fly away with them, an afternoon

767 to Charles de Gaulle, and watch the night pass in five hours, knowing she had eighteen months to escape the fat men in hotel rooms, or find another Nick. But the next morning she'd stand where the Trocadero Steps halved, looking east into the late-morning cold and trying to name the special gray of the Seine bridges. She'd decide on a top-floor apartment, three rooms with a balcony and nineteenth-century skylights, some Restoration colonnade between Sacré Coeur and the cemetery where the brick streets ran uphill. If there were tall windows, she'd never stand in them.

From the darkness, beneath the bed, the gray tomcat was two lit eyes. Annie called to him over the Brubeck while the wind jumped and guttered the candle flames. His eyes turned orange while she thought about the cop, then told herself she might become a hooker again after trying the world, something that would make him kill.

When Annie whistled for the cat with dry lips, she heard limp air, and the cat remained yellow eyes.

Her new uncle carried her to the boat while the waves took her face underwater. She left her eyes open and looked for her cats. She'd once dreamed them riding the backs of spearfish, their ears reared from the motion. Now, in her new uncle's arms, she imagined something before it happened, and each time the sea washed her face, she waited to see the cats riding fish like the cigarette cowboys did horses in her father's *Playboy* magazines from the war.

The boat was long and short, a fishing jig. She looked at the two sampans tied to the sides, then the people, a hundred shadows standing back-against-stomach, and knew her father was among them. He got stuck in the middle and couldn't see her to call. Annie's new uncle, a man who was only hands in the water, understood her father was trapped in the middle, but remained quiet, never telling her for certain because he might scare her cats. They were waiting behind the boat, the fish they rode like standing horses, and her uncle was afraid to speak.

When the waves calmed, the wind chilled Annie's eyeballs, and she nestled into her uncle, searching for his heat, but the water swirled between them and took away his hard touch, making him like the sea. The boat teetered after the wind, and the people gasped until it righted, then coughed and spoke in low tones until the gusts came again. The cats must stay underwater because it was warmer.

Her uncle came upon the boat while the water calmed. It made sounds when the people reached for her, water lapping wood. She watched the silent faces, then lay back and smiled. If they'd stop reaching, the boat would steady, and she'd hear her cats laughing from the backs of the spearfish. She'd have her father tell them. When her uncle lifted her into the wind, she went numb and hoped a coughing person wouldn't get her.

The woman got Annie by reaching the farthest for her. She took her beneath the armpits, and lifted her from her uncle, and his hands gave way very fast. The woman's eyes were dark like her black *ao dai*. When Annie came into the boat from the sea, dripping in the night, the people were still reaching overboard for her, and she couldn't hear her giggling cats. The woman sounded breathless, her face a shadow, and Annie looked past into the crowd, hoping to see her father. He'd make them stop tipping the boat.

Annie stood on the wet wood and kept looking. She wished it was morning, time for mangoes and bananas with coconut milk. Then, she could see her father because he always cut the fruit.

The woman had a little boy with a piece of jade around his neck. He wore silk pajamas, blue like rainy nights, and he faced her without smiling, touching her hips before kissing her. He ran his fingers up her thighs. The woman was laughing.

"A little wife for you," she said.

He pressed his tongue against Annie's teeth. She couldn't see past his eyeballs.

"You know how to love her very well," the woman said.

The people had stopped reaching and the boat calmed. The boy pulled their stomachs together while Annie closed her eyes and listened for the cats.

Annie held the plank, three minutes now, her shoulder blades splaying open. The gray cat's tail swept her face while he licked the puddled sweat off the floor. It covered her mirrored nose, looking like a candy cane. When she blew the tail, a slow exhale, the cat reared his ears and looked behind himself, before running into her bedroom.

In the mirror, Goetzler's head poked through the kitchen window, She rolled against the wall and assumed a yoga squat. She'd escape from her bedroom window and slide down the gray stones to the muddy grass. Her cat would be safe, hiding under the bed until she got the broomstick. She eyed Goetzler in the mirror before she moved.

His legs teetered and he couldn't touch the floor. His belt buckle had stuck against the sill. He grabbed the radiator, burning himself, but remained quiet, fanning his palm in the dark room. The pistol fell away and spun across the linoleum, lodging beneath the refrigerator. Annie jumped and went for the gun. Goetzler reached for her like he was swimming.

She put her finger over her lips.

He looked at her with the .38, blinking his eyes twice, then burned his palm on the radiator again.

"Just teeter," she said.

He didn't know where to put his hands.

"You will keep meeting me," she said. "Do you think I am alone?"

"No," he said.

"But you came here to kill me?"

"I can't talk like this," he said.

"You can always talk, Goetzler."

He was silent.

"If you killed me," she lied, "you wouldn't have gotten home."

"I wanted my life," he said.

"You'll live," she said. "I'll live."

His glasses slid down his nose. Annie knew he couldn't breathe well enough to talk.

"There's a picture of this wounded marine near the DMZ," she said. "Larry Burrows took it. He's reaching out to another wounded man who's sitting in the mud. The other marines won't let him."

Goetzler tried resting his toes on the fire escape.

"Stop," she said.

He resumed teetering. The radiator steam made his face red and fogged his glasses. She watched him burn his same hand three times.

"The marine has a bloody bandage tied beneath his chin," she said. "The hills had been swallowing them for weeks, but the men stop him from reaching out. Do you remember the picture? The day looked steamy from the sun after the rain."

Goetzler tried balancing himself by outstretching his arms and legs. The sweat ran from his scalp into his eyes.

"I want you to go outside," she said. "Then stand in the mud between the sidewalk and the street. Make like the marine who tried reaching out. Remember, there are men watching you on the street. If you don't do it, you won't make it home."

When he slid backward, Annie cocked the hammer, and the sound of the cylinder locking turned him still.

"If you were Vietnamese," she said, "what you did with the pictures could have worked."

He rocked on his lower stomach, his lips open, his teeth wet. His palms kept hitting the radiator.

"Remember that you are wanting to help," she said. "But the other men say no. The hills are swallowing you all."

He let his toes touch the fire escape, then kicked back into the air. His glasses went to the end of his nose.

"How long?" Goetzler had sucked air through his nose to talk.

"Until you figure out why they never let the wounded marines touch."

Sweat stuck the white hair to his forehead. Annie now held the pistol with both hands.

"Thursday at Marche," she said. "One o'clock. Meet my cab. Sixty thousand."

When Goetzler backed through the window, he came down hard on his knees. The frame cut his scalp. He looked at her before pushing the glasses up, his eyes like a scared dog's, then his toes touched the fire escape. He stood and went down the stairs, hitting every second step. Annie uncocked the hammer and exhaled hard enough to bow her legs. When she walked the hallway, she let the pistol arm swing.

Her bedroom door had been pushed open by the running cat. In passing, she looked for his eyes beneath the bed, muted yellow, but he'd gone to the middle, and wouldn't come out until she used the broom handle. He was scared under by car alarms and aerosol cans, like the cop, but the image of Goetzler stuck in the window might keep him hidden until morning. Even after the stick, the gray tom would pace the apartment while she finished the dying warrior, her last yoga position. The cat wouldn't lick the sweat from her obliques. The activity made him skittish for the night.

Annie lit candles on her way to the mirror, flaming the end table, the mantel. She fired six incense sticks, setting them in a jar before the mirror, then lay the silenced .38 beside the rice mat and thought of new leaves on Parisian plain trees.

27

The airport limo was coming for Mike Spence in a half hour. He'd ride to O'Hare in a four-door Lincoln town car, bound for Zihuatanejo, Mexico, and ignore the complimentary *Sun-Times* and *Tribune* on the seat behind the Serb driver. He couldn't live in a city without a decent newspaper. Instead, he'd read *The New York Times*, some obituary about a chess champion who was unknown to Mike, and sip Fiji water while the cell-talking driver moved through the late Kennedy traffic by using the shoulder. James Taylor might even be singing on 93.9 Lite FM: *Oh, Mexico, it sounds so sweet with the sun sinking low.* From the street, Mike knew cops often listened to the Lite to ward off panic attacks.

Maybe he'd feel like a writer on the ride to the airport and life again would have the theme music of a movie. If he missed nothing else about the two years he wrote, it was being able to elevate his movement through life by imagining theme music. There was AC/DC for the army, Radiohead for Susan and his last year together, and Bill Evans for all the lost ideas of himself. Things always felt more poignant and resolvable. But now, the car was twenty minutes away, and Mike was standing among his life packed into boxes, unsure of the right song. He stared at the wool blanket hiding the woman's window from his eyes. After taking a beating, Mike still didn't trust himself to look away.

He sat on his suitcase and looked at the blanket. It was Mike's barracks bedspread, green and wool, and he noticed two small holes. The streetlight was leaking through them in narrow slants. He realized the army had been long ago, and he saw Dilger beaten only because he was there. He could have witnessed a rape in a fraternity house, and hated himself into manhood for thinking assholes were ever his brothers.

Let it go, he thought. Breathe the way you are supposed to.

But turning from the window, he looked at the blinds shadowed on the oak floor, and saw a cat print on the oak floor. He started talking out loud instead of breathing.

You would not know the place, Susan.

I knocked down the whole wall two months after you were gone. You wanted French doors so the cats could print them with their paws. I just kept going with the sledge until it was all done. You are too extreme, you'd say. I knew I'd come to care nothing about what you thought. You would walk off and close the porch door and pet cats and cry among the windows and the city dark.

I picked up plaster and cracked wall studs for two days. I lay with the rubble the first night, wound in the Indian blanket on one mattress. The cold wind fogged the windows and I could not see out. I then kept my eyes closed.

You have come to my dreams since you died and you smile in the warm rain between dripping trees and I know that somehow you are fine. But that is only in the dream. When I wake and stand in our window, the morning dark windy and furious between the trees, I know that I could never find you again. Sometimes my knees go and I hold the wall.

Mike went quiet long enough for a small rain to start. When the drops became cyclic against the window, the limo honked for him the way the dispatcher had said. Don't worry if you miss the horn, the accented guy told Mike, the driver will call you on his cell phone. Please know that we take care of everything between the door and the terminal. Mike stood up with his two suitcases, wondering how much they charged hourly to care for him beyond the airport gate.

He didn't think about Susan when he walked down the stairs. His suitcases were large in the tight space and he focused upon not scratching the walls. His wife would always be alive, and he needed to figure ways to forgive himself for never knowing how to love her that last year. In Mexico, he could change the way he remembered her. He'd take them back to when they tried reinventing love with water sex and warm wind, then forget the two years afterward by filling steno pads with the memories. He'd write without hope or despair, sitting in a lounge beside a plate of orange peelings, and then kayak in the Pacific so he'd come closer to something he felt more than he understood. *Oh, Mexico, it sounds so sweet with the sun sinking low.*

His plan might go off like a pop song. Mexico in the morning dark could forever change the image the time of day brought to his mind: gentle, solitary gray light without the slaggy air left by late-night traffic, or the crows that scavenge the cold gutter leaves before dawn. He'd see the wind in palm leaves, not bare hickory branches, and the sun rising behind the ocean would never get lost in the black clouds blown down from Wisconsin. After running in the Pacific morning dark for two weeks, the beach appearing from the receding tide beneath his Teva sandals, he'd forget what Chicago looked like in the moments before dawn.

Mike wheeled the suitcases out the front door. It was colder than three hours ago when he came back from the real estate agency. Every other streetlight was dark, and the rain slanting through the lit lamps was on the verge of becoming snow. The Lincoln idled in the street and the trunk was open, but the driver stood inside his open door. Mike pulled his luggage to the sidewalk and saw that the driver was gray and Balkan. He laughed before he looked back at Mike.

"There's a nutball here," he said. "Look at him."

Mike pitched his luggage inside the trunk. His eighteen months as a cop taught him to ignore anybody who drove professionally. Ambulance drivers and cabbies would talk like channels flipping on a Sony thirty-six-inch television, and this driver rambled with the same visual bytes. Mike wanted to leave Claremont Avenue like he'd snuff out a candle, then walk down the airplane steps into the Mexican white light and ocean-smelling wind. There was pain to bury with his kayak paddle into the blue Pacific waves. There were steno pads to fill and pencils to sharpen.

When he closed the trunk, the driver was pointing at a thin, gray man standing in the mud. His legs were splitting while his arms raised at the elbows. He reached out with small fingers, straining as if leashed, his eyes dead-set. He wanted to lay his small hands on something. The driver looked at Mike and nodded while he smiled around his rodent nose.

"This mad bastard won't move," he said. "You can tell him that his mother has balls and he won't say a word. Why don't you try?"

The driver grinned and pointed at the man. He waited for Mike to speak, nodding with great enthusiasm.

"Go on," the driver said, "say his mother dances in the nursing home for pop-machine money."

Mike realized that Annie was giving up her john. If this guy got a flat tire, people would drive by without noticing. The driver was laughing in the rain, and pointing harder for Mike to talk. This was nothing to see.

"You can't give this up," he said. "You can say anything to this goofy bastard. Tell him that his father likes boys."

Mike tried to get into the john's eyes, but the man was looking permanently away. He was beyond the three-flat roofs, even the sky made starless by the city lights. He didn't even have a face. But Mike didn't connect him to the killer until he recognized his stance from Larry Burrows's picture "Reaching Out," the famous shot of a post-battle marine rifle squad in the hills outside Khe Sanh. This john was the tall black marine stiff like a stunned boxer while they kept him from his wounded buddy. He was exact about holding himself back.

This hooker was sadistic. She wanted the john to understand that his options had vanished by using a Vietnam War picture against him.

Feel powerlessness, round-eye, the hooker said. You cannot touch what you think needs your help.

Mike walked and kept the car between himself and this mime-like john. The man saw him, but wouldn't meet his eyes. The driver was pointing and laughing.

"Let's go to the airport," Mike said. "My *New York Times* is getting wet."

The driver looked at Mike with unbelieving eyes.

"Why don't you want to tell this zapped asshole to fuck off and die?" he said. "He won't even move. You can let the crazy prick have it."

Mike got inside the warm Lincoln. He opened his paper on his knees, but hadn't looked at it. He took the Fiji water from his coat pocket. The only thing missing was a moving car.

"What could I say," Mike said. "You took all the best words."

The driver sat down and closed his door. He seemed calmer.

"I do pick good combinations of curse words," the driver said. "I am hard to beat."

Mike watched the john stand in the new snow and reach out while the car passed the street. The driver was green in the dash light and Mike noticed candle flames illuming the hooker's windows. He let himself believe the sun hadn't muddied the coral reefs outside Zihuatanejo. When he met eyes with the driver in the rearview mirror, the man seemed unnerved by Mike's silence.

"I drove a cab in four countries," he said, "but Lincolns in America. I can curse in four languages better than any whore. I also read three newspapers a day. I am in the streets, but I am not of them."

Mike Spence held his laughter when he noticed the driver was playing Lite FM. Neil Young sang slowly, his voice like sunlit regret, but Mike couldn't hear enough to know the exact song.

"I bet you always know right what to say," he said to the driver.